Yukio Mishima

LIFE FOR SALE

Yukio Mishima was born in Tokyo in 1925. He graduated from Tokyo Imperial University's School of Jurisprudence in 1947. His first published book, *The Forest in Full Bloom,* appeared in 1944, and he established himself as a major author with *Confessions of a Mask* (1949). From then until his death, he continued to publish novels, short stories, and plays each year. His crowning achievement, The Sea of Fertility tetralogy—which contains the novels *Spring Snow* (1969), *Runaway Horses* (1969), *The Temple of Dawn* (1970), and *The Decay of the Angel* (1971)—is considered one of the definitive works of twentieth-century Japanese fiction. In 1970, at the age of forty-five and the day after completing the last novel in the Fertility series, Mishima committed seppuku (ritual suicide)—a spectacular death that attracted worldwide attention.

ALSO BY YUKIO MISHIMA

THE SEA OF FERTILITY, A CYCLE OF FOUR NOVELS

Spring Snow

Runaway Horses

The Temple of Dawn

The Decay of the Angel

Confessions of a Mask

Thirst for Love

Forbidden Colors

The Sailor Who Fell from Grace with the Sea

After the Banquet

The Temple of the Golden Pavilion

Five Modern Nō Plays

The Sound of Waves

Death in Midsummer

Acts of Worship

The Frolic of the Beasts

LIFE FOR SALE

Yukio Mishima

Translated from the Japanese
by Stephen Dodd

Vintage International
VINTAGE BOOKS
A DIVISION OF PENGUIN RANDOM HOUSE LLC
NEW YORK

A VINTAGE INTERNATIONAL ORIGINAL, APRIL 2020

Library of Congress Cataloging-in-Publication Data
Names: Mishima, Yukio, 1925–1970, author. | Dodd, Stephen, 1955– translator.
Title: Life for sale / Yukio Mishima ; translated from the Japanese by Stephen Dodd.
Other titles: Inochi urimasu. English
Description: First U.S. edition. | New York : Vintage Books, 2020.
Identifiers: LCCN 2019032426 (print) | LCCN 2019032427 (ebook) | ISBN 9780525565147 (trade paperback) | ISBN 9780525565154 (ebook)
Classification: LCC PL833.I7 I513 2020 (print) | LCC PL833.I7 (ebook) | DDC 895.63/5—dc23
LC record available at https://lccn.loc.gov/2019032426

Vintage International Trade Paperback ISBN: 978-0-525-56514-7
eBook ISBN: 978-0-525-56515-4

www.vintagebooks.com

Printed in the United States of America
10 9 8 7

LIFE FOR SALE

1

. . . When Hanio regained consciousness, everything around him dazzled so brightly he thought he might be in heaven. But a splitting headache lingered at the back of his skull. Surely there were no headaches in heaven.

The first thing that came into view was a large frosted-glass window. The window was featureless, and it overflowed with whiteness.

"Looks like he's come round," someone said.

"Thank goodness for that! Saving someone's life always puts a spring in your step for the rest of the day."

Hanio raised his eyes. Standing before him were a nurse and a stocky man in a paramedic's uniform.

"Come on, now. Calm down. Now is no time to be thrashing around." The nurse went to hold him down by his shoulders.

It dawned on Hanio that his attempt at suicide had failed.

He had consumed a large amount of sedative on the last overground train that evening. To be precise, he gulped it down at a drinking fountain in the station before boarding the train. And no sooner had he stretched out on the empty seats than everything went blank.

Suicide was not something he had put much thought into. He considered it likely that his sudden urge to die arose that evening while he was reading the newspaper—the edition for

November 29—at the bar where he normally ate dinner. It contained the run-of-the-mill sort of stuff, of no special significance. All the articles left him totally cold:

Ministry of Foreign Affairs Official Is a Spy
Three Places Raided, Including Japan–China Amity Association
Secretary McNamara Transfer: Final Decision
Smog Covers Metropolitan Area: First Winter Warning
Haneda Airport Explosion: Prosecution Seek No-Limit Sentence for Aono's "Heinous Crime"
Truck Plunges onto Railway Track, Collides with Goods Wagon
Transplant Success: Girl Receives Aortic Valve from Deceased Donor
¥900,000 Snatched: Robbers Steal from Kagoshima Bank Branch Office

It must have been after reading these that he had hit on the idea of suicide, as if he were planning a picnic. If he were forced to come up with a reason, he could only conclude that he had attempted to end it all on a complete whim.

He was not suffering as the result of some romantic break-up. And even if his heart had been broken, Hanio was not the type to take his own life. Nor did he have any serious financial problems at the time. He worked as a copywriter, and the jingle in that TV commercial for Goshiki Pharmaceuticals' "Fresh and Clear" digestive aid was one of his: "Fresh and Clear. Couldn't be simpler. Cured before you know it."

People considered him talented enough to strike out on his own, but he lacked any desire to do so. He worked for a company called Tokyo Ad, and the salary they paid him was good enough. Until the previous day, he had personified the honest, hardworking company employee.

But when he really thought about it, maybe there *was* a

reason why the idea of suicide had come to him. He had been skimming through the evening paper with such little concentration that the inside page slithered right down under the table.

He watched it go, the way an indolent snake might observe its old skin, just shed. The next moment he felt the urge to pick up the page. He could have left it lying there. Perhaps it was social convention that compelled him to retrieve it, or maybe he was driven by a more serious determination to restore order in the world. He was not exactly sure. In any case, he stooped under the small, wobbly table and stretched out his hand.

Just then, his eyes encountered something hideous. On top of the fallen paper was a cockroach, absolutely still. At the very moment he stretched out his hand, the glossy mahogany-colored insect scurried away with extraordinary vitality and lost itself among the printed words.

He picked up the paper nevertheless, placed the page he had been reading on the table and cast his eyes over it again. Suddenly, all the letters he was trying to make out turned into cockroaches. His eyes pursued the letters as they made their escape, their disgustingly shiny dark-red backs in full view.

"So the world boils down to nothing more than this."

It was a sudden revelation. And it was this insight that led to an overwhelming desire to die.

But upon further reflection, he found this explanation just a little too pat. Surely things were not so clear-cut. We just have to soldier on, even if every word in the newspaper is reduced to a string of cockroaches. It was in reaction to this thought that the idea of "death" finally lodged itself in his mind. From that moment, death hung over him, snugly, the way snow caps a red postbox after a particularly heavy snowfall.

This change in attitude produced some improvement in his

spirits. He went into a pharmacy to buy the sedative, but was not quite ready to swallow it down immediately, so he went to watch a triple feature at the movies. When he emerged, he dropped by a pick-up bar where he occasionally hung out.

The dumpy girl sitting next to him exuded such an overall impression of dullness that he was not tempted in the slightest. Even so, he was afflicted by an urge to confess that he was about to kill himself. He gave her ample elbow a little nudge with his own. The girl stole a glance at him, then lazily turned toward him on her chair as if it required a huge effort. She had the laugh of a country bumpkin.

"Good evening," said Hanio.

"Good evening."

"You're pretty."

She giggled.

"Do you know what I'm going to say next?"

She giggled again.

"You can't tell, can you?"

"Well, I might have an idea."

"Later on tonight, I intend to kill myself."

Far from being shocked, the girl let out a broad guffaw. She tossed a strip of dried squid right into her mouth, and continued to chew for ages even as she laughed. The stench of the squid clung to the region around Hanio's nose.

Before long, someone, apparently a friend of hers, turned up and the girl waved affectedly in her direction. She disentangled herself from Hanio's side without so much as a nod.

Hanio also left the bar, alone and curiously irritated that his intention to die had failed to make an impression. The evening was still young, but the appeal of the "last train" was fixed in his mind, so he had to think of a way to pass the time. He went into a pachinko parlor and started playing at one of the slot machines. He won tons of balls. A human life was about to end, but the balls kept pouring forth in an endless stream. It felt as if someone was making fun of him.

Finally, it was time for the last train.

Hanio passed through the ticket barrier, slugged down the sedative at the drinking fountain and boarded the train.

2

Now that Hanio had failed to commit suicide, a wonderfully free and empty world opened up before him.

From that day on, he made a complete break with the daily grind he had always believed would go on forever. He felt that the world was his for the taking. The days would no longer merge into one. Each day would expire, one after the other. He could see it all clearly before him: a row of dead frogs with their white bellies exposed.

He handed in his resignation to Tokyo Ad. The company's business was booming, so they gave him a substantial severance payment. This provided him with a lifestyle that left him beholden to no one.

He placed the following advertisement in the Situations Wanted column of a tabloid newspaper: "Life for Sale. Use me as you wish. I am a twenty-seven-year-old male. Discretion guaranteed. Will cause no bother at all."

He added his apartment address, and then stuck a slip of paper onto his front door with the following written on it:

Hanio Yamada—Life for Sale

The first day, not one person came to his door. But ever since he had stopped work, Hanio was never at a loss about how to fill the empty hours. He would lounge around his one-room apartment watching television, or lose himself in daydreams.

When the ambulance had brought him to Accident and Emergency, he was out cold, so you would have expected him to have no recollection of what had happened that night. But strangely, the wail of an ambulance siren brought an unmistakable memory of his ride flooding back. He was stretched out on the gurney snoring loudly. A paramedic in a white gown sat beside him, holding the blanket down in order to prevent the violent lurching of the vehicle from throwing his body from the bed. He saw it as clear as day. The paramedic had a big mole right by the side of his nose . . .

And yet how empty this new life felt, like a room without furniture.

The following morning, there was a knock on the door of the apartment. Hanio opened it to find a small, neatly dressed old man who, after a few furtive backward glances, hastily entered and shut the door behind him.

"I assume you are Mr. Hanio Yamada?"

"That is correct."

"I saw your ad in the newspaper."

"Oh, please come through."

Hanio led him inside to a corner of the red-carpeted room that he had furnished with a black table and chairs, the kind you might expect to see in the home of someone employed in the design world.

The old man issued a cobra-like hiss through his teeth as he politely bowed and took a seat.

"So you're the one whose life is for sale?"

"Yes, I am."

"Well, you're obviously young, and making a decent living. What makes you want to do this?"

"Don't ask things that don't concern you."

"Even so . . . How much are you selling your life for?"

"That depends on how much you are willing to give."

"That's highly irresponsible of you. Surely you should set your own price on what your life is worth. What would you do if I offered one hundred yen?"

"If that's what you want, it's fine by me."

"Come on, that's a ridiculous thing to say."

The old man took out a wallet from his breast pocket and produced five crisp-looking ten-thousand-yen notes. He spread them out in the shape of a fan as if they were playing cards.

There was no emotion in Hanio's eyes as he pocketed the fifty thousand yen. "You can tell me anything you like. I won't be offended."

"OK." The old man took out some filtered cigarettes. "You get lung cancer if you smoke these. Fancy one? I don't suppose a man who is selling his life worries about cancer?

"It's a very simple matter. My wife—well, actually, she's my third—is now twenty-three years old. There is exactly half a century in age between us. She's a magnificent woman, you know. Her breasts—they point in different directions, like two doves miffed with each other. And her lips are sweet and full, pouting and inviting. I can't begin to describe how amazing her body is. And she has great legs. There seems to be a fashion now for women to have abnormally slender legs. Too slender, if you ask me. But hers taper off ever so gently from her fleshy thighs, all the way down to her ankles. It's hard to find the right words. Her buttocks are shaped like little mounds that remind you of molehills.

"Well, she's left me, and she's doing the rounds with whoever takes her fancy. Right now, she's shacked up with some shady Asian guy—a Chinese or a Korean. He's a mobster, but not your ordinary, run-of-the-mill mobster. He's the owner of no fewer than four restaurants, and I'm sure he's knocked off a couple of people in turf wars.

"What I'm asking is that you acquaint yourself with my wife, become intimate and make sure that this mobster finds the pair of you at it. When he claps eyes on you, you're sure to get killed, and she'll probably be dead meat too. Well? That's my way of getting even . . . That's all there is to it. Could you manage to die like that for me?"

"I see." Hanio listened, affecting an air of indifference. Then he asked: "But I wonder if it will have such a romantic ending? I appreciate you're dreaming about taking revenge on your wife, but what if she's more than willing to die a happy death because she's with me?"

"She's definitely not the kind of woman with a death wish. She's different from you in that sense. She wants to squeeze every last drop she can get out of life. It's as if every fiber of her body has been written through with some sort of magic spell."

"What makes you say that?"

"You'll know soon enough. In any event, I would appreciate a neat death. I assume a written agreement is unnecessary?"

"That's right; it won't be required."

More hissing sounds emerged from the old man's lips. He was clearly mulling things over. "Is there anything you'd like me to make arrangements for after your death?"

"No, not particularly. I don't want a funeral, and I don't need a grave. But there is one thing that maybe you could do for me. I've always wanted to keep a Siamese cat as a pet, but I've never got around to it. So after I'm dead, I'd be grateful if you could get one and take care of it on my behalf. In my mind, I envisage you letting it drink milk from a large ladle rather than a saucer. After it laps up the first couple of mouthfuls, you should give the ladle a slight flip so that the milk splashes up and the cat's face gets a good soaking. It would be good if you could do that once a day. This is really important, so I'd like you not to forget."

"What a weird thing to ask!"

"You only think that because you inhabit an exceptionally ordinary world. A request like this is way beyond your powers of imagination. Before I forget, if I happen to come back alive, does the fifty thousand yen have to be returned?"

"It just won't happen. All I ask is that you make sure my wife bites the bullet when the moment arises."

"So it's a murder contract."

"I guess so. Look, I just want to ensure that we rub out every trace of her from this world. What I don't want is to feel any guilt. It's just not worth putting myself through the mill, and then feeling remorseful on top of that . . . So, we're agreed. I'd like you to get started tonight. I'll pay incidental expenses whenever you make a claim."

"Where do I go to 'get started'?"

"Here's a map. It's Apartment 865 in this fancy apartment block at the top of the hill called Villa Borghese. I believe it's the penthouse on the top floor. I have no idea when she'll be in. Beyond that, you'll just have to play it by ear."

"What's your wife's name?"

"Ruriko Kishi. Ruriko is written in simple hiragana script. Kishi is the same Chinese character used by Prime Minister Kishi in his name." The old man looked strangely radiant as he spoke.

3

The old man turned to leave. But scarcely had he stepped out of the door than he was back again. The words that followed were entirely to be expected from someone who had purchased another's life.

"Ah, I forgot something important. You must tell no one. Not only that I'm your client, but also about your mission.

After all, you're selling your life, so a certain level of commercial decorum is involved."

"You have nothing to fear on that point."

"So you really won't sign a written oath?"

"Don't be ridiculous. To do that would be tantamount to making a public declaration of our arrangement!"

"I see what you mean."

The old man was clearly troubled as he shuffled back into the room, still hissing through his ill-fitting false teeth.

"In which case, how can I trust you?"

"Those who believe, believe everything, while those who doubt don't believe a thing. Look, you've come and given me money, haven't you? That leaves me convinced that such a thing as trust still exists in the world. And anyway, even if I were to publicize the mission you've entrusted me with, I don't have a clue who you are or where you come from. Doesn't that give you peace of mind?"

"Don't be dumb! Ruriko will spill the beans. I know that for sure."

"Maybe she will. But I'm not the blabbing kind."

"I can see that. I've known a lot of people over the years. The moment I clapped eyes on you, I knew you'd fit the bill. If you need any more money, leave me a message on the information board at the Central Exit of Shinjuku Station. Short and sweet will do. 'Waiting for money, eight o'clock tomorrow morning. Life.' Something like that.

"I like to take a stroll around the department stores every day, but it's all a bit boring before opening time. So if you want to meet during the morning, earlier is better."

The old man turned to go. As he stepped out of the door, Hanio was right behind him.

"Where are you off to?" the old man inquired.

"Obvious, isn't it? Apartment 865, Villa Borghese."

"Now that's what I call keen."

Hanio remembered to turn over the card on the door on which he had written "Life for Sale." On the other side was the single word "Sold."

4

Villa Borghese was a white, Italianate building that dominated the hill in a squalid part of town. You couldn't miss it, so there was no need for Hanio to consult the map.

He peeped through the reception window, but the concierge was not in his chair. The hallway was deserted, so he made a beeline for the elevator, visible at the rear. He walked involuntarily as if pulled by a thread, bemused by an incongruous sense of cheerful irresponsibility as a man about to commit suicide. His life overflowed with lightness.

He reached the eighth floor, where the corridor was enveloped in the deep hush of mid morning, and quickly found the door to Apartment 865. As he pushed the bell, pleasant chimes reverberated within.

Maybe they were out? But Hanio somehow knew Ruriko would be at home on her own that morning. Now was just the time when a kept woman, having sent her man off for the day, would be back in bed sound asleep. It was this thought that kept Hanio's finger pressed firmly on the bell.

Finally there were signs of someone coming to the door. When it opened, the chain lock was still attached to its track: the bemused face of a young woman peered through the gap. She was wearing a nightdress, but showed no sign of having just woken up. Her expression was vivid and sharply focused. Sure enough, her lips pouted invitingly.

"Who are you?"

"I'm from Life for Sale. I wonder if you might be interested in life insurance?"

"Thank you, but we have lots already. We don't need any more insurance."

The fact that, despite her blunt words, she did not immediately shut the door in his face convinced him that her interest must be piqued. He had already employed the salesman's trick of wedging a foot in the doorway.

"I don't have to come in. I would just like you to hear me out. It won't take a moment."

"No, my husband will get mad at me. And besides, I'm not presentable right now."

"Well then, I'll come again, in twenty minutes' time."

"Let me think . . ." She was mulling it over. "Why don't you go and make some other calls, then ring my bell again in twenty minutes?"

"Thank you. I'll do that." He withdrew his foot, and she closed the door.

Hanio sat on a sofa by a window at the end of the corridor and waited for twenty minutes. From there, he commanded a view of the neighborhood bathed in winter sunshine. In the bright light it was all too clear that the area was distinctly the worse for wear, as if nibbled away by termites. Of course, the locals would not fail to keep up appearances, addressing each other with a "Good morning," or asking how work was going, or inquiring into the health of their wives and children. Or they might remark on the ratcheting up of the international situation. But none of them would notice the sheer banality of their words.

After smoking a couple of cigarettes, he went and knocked again. This time the door was flung open and the woman, now dressed in a light-green suit with a splayed collar, courteously invited him in.

"Would you like tea? Or something stronger?"

"You're treating me very well for a door-to-door salesman."

"There's no way you're in insurance. I could tell the moment I saw you. If you're going to put on an act, you need to do it a bit better than that."

"Fair enough. In which case, could I trouble you for a beer?"

Ruriko laughed with a twinkle in her eye and sashayed across the room, drawing attention to her hips, which were quite wide, despite the slimness of her figure. She disappeared into the kitchen.

Presently, the pair were clinking beer glasses at the living-room table.

"So, who on earth are you?" asked Ruriko.

"Let's just say I am the milkman."

"You're teasing me. Still, I assume you knew of the risks you're taking when you came here."

"No."

"So, who asked you to come?"

"Nobody."

"That is strange. So you're telling me that you rang the bell on the off-chance that a regular glamour-puss like me might be at home?"

"That just about sums it up."

"You're a lucky man. Now, I'm afraid I don't have any nibbles. I wonder if it's odd to have chips with beer so early in the morning. Ah, I think there should be some cheese."

She hurried off to search the refrigerator again.

"Ooh, that's cold." Her voice carried from the other room. She returned with a dish of salad, with something dark on the lettuce leaves. "Do help yourself."

For some reason, though, she approached him from the rear. The next moment, something icy cold was jabbed into Hanio's cheek from behind. A single glance told him it was a gun. He was not particularly surprised.

"I bet that's freezing," she said.

"It certainly is. Do you keep it in the fridge?"

"I do, because I *hate* warm weapons."

"You're quite the fussy one, aren't you?"

"Aren't you afraid?"

"Not particularly."

"You think you can play with me because I'm a woman. But look, I'm going to give you plenty of time to fess up, so drink your beer and say your prayers."

Ruriko cautiously withdrew the gun and walked all the way round him to sit on the chair opposite. The gun remained cocked and pointed in his direction. Hanio held the beer glass in his hand, which remained absolutely steady. But what intrigued him was the faint quiver in Ruriko's hand.

"That's quite some disguise you've got there," she said. "I bet you're Chinese or Korean. How many years have you been in Japan?"

"Give me a break. I'm a Japanese, the genuine article."

"Liar! You're snooping for my husband. I know it. I bet your real name is Kin or Li, or something like that."

"May I ask what you base this delusion of yours upon?"

"You're a cool one. So you're not going to be straight with me . . . In which case, I guess my only choice is to spell out once more what I'm sure you already know. My husband is jealous as hell, and last night I was under suspicion yet again for no reason at all. I was in a really sticky situation, but in the end he arranged for his goon to keep an eye on me. Even so, it wasn't enough for him just to keep watch from a distance. He's testing me, I know—getting someone to sneak into the house to try and seduce me, isn't he? Well, I won't have it. Take one step my way and I'll shoot.

"But come to think of it, he was the one who gave me a gun for my own protection, and it was he who made a point of ensuring I could use it properly . . . You know, it might just be that you've been roped into something completely unawares. Maybe you're the one who's fallen into a trap . . . I bet you had no idea that you've been selected for the role of getting yourself bumped off by me so I can prove what a virtuous woman I am."

"You don't say." Hanio played it cool, and looked her straight in the eye. "Well, if I'm going to be killed anyway, I'd prefer to sleep together first. If we do, I promise I won't kick up any fuss when you kill me afterward."

Ruriko's gradually rising fury flared across Hanio's field of vision. It was like reading a map where the contour lines suddenly bunch together.

"I've heard that before. You might even be from the ACS."

"ACS—is that the name of a TV station?"

"Don't play cute with me. I'm talking about the Asia Confidential Service."

"You've completely lost me now."

"But of course, I almost fell for it! I very nearly killed someone, and that would have landed me in my husband's clutches for the rest of my life. He's dreamt up some romantic scheme to get me back as his little floozy, hasn't he? First he arranges for me to protect my virtue by killing someone. And since he's one of only five people in Japan capable of giving shelter to killers, he intends to keep me under lock and key for the rest of my days. Now that's scary. If you really are from the ACS, tell me now."

Convinced she had hit the nail on the head, Ruriko flung the gun onto the cushion next to her. "You should've said earlier that you were from the ACS."

That name again. Rather than deny it, Hanio decided to play along.

"So you're one of his stooges, too, are you?" Ruriko went on. "And your cover was a 'life insurance' alias. I had no idea. In that case, even he might have let me into it beforehand. But what an appalling actor you are! You must be new to the ACS, right? How many months' training have you received?"

"Six months."

"That's not very long. So you managed to get fluent in all those Southeast Asian languages, including all the Chinese dialects, in such a short time?"

"Uh-huh." He was reduced to giving nothing but vague responses.

"Still, you've shown some real guts. I'm impressed."

Ruriko's expression relaxed. She stood up and went to gaze out over the balcony, where there was a garden chair, its white paint peeling, with a garden table of the same design. Rain from the previous day still clung in quivering drops from the edge of the table top.

"So how many pounds did he ask you to transport?"

Stumped by what to say, Hanio replied, "I can't tell you that." And then he yawned.

"After all, the gold in Laos is dirt cheap. With the Vientiane market price as it is, you would at least double your profits if you brought it to Tokyo. A previous ACS man did something really clever. He dissolved gold in nitro-hydrochloric acid, and brought it in as a dozen bottles of Scotch whisky. Then he turned it back into gold. Can you imagine that?"

"Sounds very far-fetched to me. Yeah, the shoes I'm wearing today look like crocodile skin, but underneath what's visible to the eye, they're actually gold. My feet feel quite cold."

"Those shoes, you mean?"

Ruriko leaned over to examine Hanio's feet with unalloyed curiosity, but she saw no trace of any weighty, glittering gold. Meanwhile, Hanio's eyes were drawn like a magnet to the deep cleft between her breasts, which, ill-partnered though they were, pressed urgently against each other in that valley of powdered whiteness. They did indeed "point in different directions," as the old man had said. Ruriko seemed to have applied talc to the region. A kiss there would be like burying your nose in baby powder. Hanio could well imagine.

"So tell me, how do you go about importing American weapons into Japan via Laos?" Ruriko went on. "Do you have to make a stopover in Hong Kong? That's a real pain. Surely it'd be much simpler to go to the military base in Tachikawa and get some there—that place is chock-a-block with weapons from America."

Hanio cut in with a question of his own: "By the way, what time does your husband get back?"

"He'll drop by for a while around lunchtime. Didn't he tell you?"

"Well, I timed it to get here a bit early. So, how about having a little lie-down together before he actually arrives?" Hanio gave another yawn and removed his jacket.

"My, my, you are tired, aren't you? You can use my husband's bed."

"I'd much prefer yours."

Without warning, Hanio grabbed hold of Ruriko. Ruriko struggled to get out of his grasp, and in the process she managed to clutch hold of the gun with her outstretched hand.

"You fool! Do you want to get your head blown off?" she cried.

"Either way I end up dead. It's all the same to me."

"Well, that's not true for me. If I shoot you dead right now, I'll at least get away with my life. But if we're in bed together when he gets here, then it'll be curtains for the both of us."

"I know which option I'd prefer. OK, let me ask you something. Do you know what happens to a person who kills an ACS man for no reason?"

Ruriko turned pale and shook her head.

"This."

Hanio strode up to the display shelf and picked up a Swiss national doll. He delivered a chop to its spine, then bent the doll back so far in his hands that it snapped in two.

5

Hanio was first to strip down, and as he slipped between the sheets, he thought over the course of action he should take.

"The key is to keep it going as long as possible. The longer we're in the sack, the better the chance that her guy will burst in on us and shoot us both dead."

If they were killed in the middle of it all, that would be a great way to go. That was how he saw it. If he were old, it might be a source of shame, but for a young man there could be no greater honor than to die on the job.

Of course, the ideal was to remain entirely unaware of impending death until the instant it happened, allowing him to plunge instantaneously from the height of ecstasy to the abyss of annihilation. But for Hanio, this was simply not an option. He would have to stretch things out in the full knowledge that he was about to die. For most people the sheer terror of this thought would be a hindrance to sexual pleasure, but not so for Hanio. He would be dead even before his mouth had time to drop open in shock. And since this was not his first brush with death, it was no big deal. Until he reached that point, all that mattered was to live each moment of life as it came, to savor it fully and for as long as it lasted.

Ruriko seemed unfazed. She fiddled around with the venetian blinds, closing them partially, but left the curtains open. Then she stripped off unceremoniously in the aquarium-blue light. In the gap of the bathroom door, which she'd purposely left ajar, he got a full view of her naked form in the mirror as she sprayed perfume under her arms and dabbed some behind her ears.

The rounded contours of her shoulders and buttocks brought delicious embraces to mind. Stirred by the sight, Hanio could hardly believe what was happening.

Walking gracefully around the bed once, naked, she finally slipped in beside him.

Hanio was aware it would not constitute good pillow talk, but he could not suppress his curiosity: "Why on earth did you circle round the bed like that?"

"It's a ritual of mine. You know, dogs often do the same thing before they lie down. It's a kind of instinct."

"You're really something!"

"Come on now, we haven't got all day. Take me in your arms." Ruriko's words sounded heavy as, eyes closed, she grasped Hanio's head in her hands.

Hanio's strategy was to maintain things for as long as possible by keeping her constantly on the edge. He intended to devote lots of time to trying one thing, then go back to the starting point; to try something else, and return once more to the beginning. But once he began his first foray, he was surprised at the unexpected turn of events. Ruriko's body was certainly worthy of all the old man's deep attachment. As a result, Hanio's plan almost ended in failure, but he stood his ground.

His one concern was to ensure that Ruriko didn't get distracted, that she remained fully focused on what they were up to even as the threat of death pressed in. To this end, Hanio employed all the tricks at his disposal: by flooding her with a sense of regret that it might be about to end, by keeping her in suspense and enthralled by the knowledge that it was not over yet. He took pride in his expert ability to carve out small rest breaks for this very purpose. Ruriko's entire body flushed pink, and as she lay on the bed it was plain that she was caught in a complete limbo. She was a prisoner trying to cling desperately with her eyes to the ceiling light, only to find her attention slipping away from it again.

Hanio went on the attack, then rested; rested, then attacked again. But every effort brought him closer to falling into the beguiling trap of Ruriko's body. The only way he could avoid giving in to the moment was to try to devote all his attention to his companion's fantasies as they gradually took physical shape before him.

Vigorously applying himself to his task, Hanio heard a key turn softly in the apartment door. Ruriko noticed nothing, her eyes shut tight as she swung her faintly damp face from side to side.

"So, this is it," thought Hanio. Any second now, a gun fixed with a silencer would create a small red tunnel right through his back straight into Ruriko's chest.

He heard the sound of the door being closed softly. Someone was in the apartment, he knew that much. But nothing happened.

Hanio found it too much effort to look over his shoulder. Indeed, if this really was the last moment left to him, it seemed only right to put everything he had into it. Should death visit at that very instant, even better. It was not as if his whole life had been building up to this moment, but he made the very best of it by strenuously flinging himself into Ruriko's exquisite trap, giving full vent to the feelings of insatiable lust for this windfall of a gift. Since nothing happened even after their tremors had subsided, he arched his neck up, snake-like, and turned around, still resting on top of her body.

A fat, odd-looking man, dressed in a fancy apricot-colored jacket and sporting a beret, met his eyes. He was sitting by the table where Hanio had earlier shared a drink with Ruriko. A large sketchbook was open on his knees, and his pencil was moving furiously.

"Stay as you are. Don't move," he said gently, before shifting his gaze back to the page.

At the sound of his voice, Ruriko gave a start. Hanio was taken aback by the visceral terror in her face.

Ruriko yanked the sheet toward her, wrapping it around her body, and sat up. Completely exposed, Hanio had no option but to lie there, casting glances first at Ruriko and then at the man.

"Why didn't you shoot? Why didn't you just kill us?" Ruriko screamed, in a shrill voice. She began to sob. "Don't tell me. You're going to keep our feet to the fire, aren't you, for as long as you can."

"Don't get in a tizzy. Calm down." The man spoke Japanese in an odd accent. He threw himself even further into his pencil work and totally ignored Hanio. "I'm just making a sketch of you. I think it's going to turn out well. The way both of you moved was beautiful. I'm having an artistic moment, so both of you, just stay as you are for a bit longer, please."

Hanio and Ruriko were both rendered speechless.

6

"There. Finished." The man closed the sketchbook, removed his beret, and placed them both on the table. He went up to the bed, hands on hips as if he were a primary-school teacher admonishing a couple of kids: "Come on now, put your clothes on. You'll catch cold otherwise."

Still utterly bemused, Hanio donned the clothes he had earlier discarded with such abandon. Ruriko, wrapped in the sheet, rose indignantly to her feet and stormed into the bathroom. The sheet got caught in the door behind her, so she jerked it inside with an angry mutter. The door slammed shut.

The man spoke: "Please, join me. Do you fancy a drink?"

Hanio reluctantly joined him at the table.

"That woman takes ages getting ready. She'll be in the bathroom at least thirty minutes. We have no option but to wait. You should have a drink, then do the grown-up thing and go home."

As he spoke, the man took out a pre-bottled Manhattan mix from the fridge, daintily placed a cherry in each cocktail glass, then poured out the drink from a height. The plumpness of his hands gave the impression of boundless generosity. There were even dimples in the joints of his fingers.

"By the way, I'm not going to bother asking who you are. What difference would it make anyway?"

"Ruriko thought I might be a member of the ACS."

"You may not be aware of this, but the ACS only exists in thriller mangas. Truth be told, I'm very much a peace-loving guy—I wouldn't harm a fly. But she has a problem—she suffers from sexual frigidity. So I have to make up all sorts of scenarios in order to give her a kick and spice things up a bit. That way she's satisfied and she gets to brandish a toy gun under the illusion it's the real thing. I'm a complete pacifist at heart, you know. I think it's vital for people of every country to get along peacefully and help each other through foreign trade and commerce. It's not so much the harming of people's bodies I find objectionable, but of their hearts. That, I believe, is the key lesson humanism has to teach us. Wouldn't you agree?"

"Oh yes, absolutely." Hanio barely knew how to respond.

"But she's got no time for my pacifism. The girl craves thrills, pure and simple, and now she's hooked on thriller mangas. So I have to play along with her. We pretend I've bumped off loads of people. I fill her head with ideas like the ACS. She loves it and that helps her overcome her frigidity, so I let her remain a prisoner to her fantasies. If I really were as she imagined, well, the Japanese police are the people running the show—there's no way they'd let me get away with it, is there? But since it's for sex, I'm happy to play the gangland mobster with a predilection for murder."

"I see. But why me . . . ?"

"No need to feel guilty. You gave pleasure to Ruriko. That also puts me in your debt, so I have no reason to reproach you. Care for another drink? And then once you've finished, you'd better go straight home. And don't come here again. I'd hate to end up feeling jealous. But I managed to get a really good drawing out of what just happened. Here, take a look."

The man opened up his sketchbook. It was an example of what they call a "motion" portrait, drawn to an almost professional standard.

Though Hanio was the object of the study, even he was overwhelmed by the strangely beautiful purity of what it depicted, giving the impression of lithe young animals absorbed in an act of untrammeled ferocity. It was "motion" itself: people overflowing with pleasure, bright, engrossed in a vigorous dance. The picture gave no hint of the subtle calculations at work within Hanio's own consciousness.

"Great picture," Hanio responded in genuine admiration as he returned the sketchbook.

"Not bad, eh? When people are happy they are always at their most beautiful, I think. They're completely at peace with themselves. I have no desire to get in the way of that. It's perfection itself. I'm glad I managed to get it down on paper. Now, you should leave, before Ruriko comes out of the bathroom."

The man stood up and held out his hand. It looked so soft and squashy that Hanio was reluctant to shake it, but it was time for him to go.

"Goodbye, then," said Hanio, and moved toward the door. Just then, he felt a hand on his shoulder.

"You're still young," said the man. "You must forget everything that happened just now. You understand me, right? What went on today, right here, the people you met—you should forget it all. You get me? That way, you'll be left with nothing but good memories. Think of these words as my parting gift, to take with you for the rest of your life. Make the most of it."

7

Hanio emerged into the bright outdoors with what had struck him as extremely sound, sensible advice still ringing in his ears. Even he felt that this morning's experience was a mad fantasy. He had intended to play the nihilist until, that is, the wisdom of the older man had enlightened him: it was as if he had been instantaneously transformed into a proper adult. Until that moment, the man had been treating him with kid gloves as if he were still a child.

As he walked along the winter streets, it occurred to him that someone might be tailing him. He looked back, but there was no one there. To think that he, of all people, had been taken in by some thriller manga! And he was probably not the only one. His client, the old man with the hiss, had probably fallen for it too.

A new snack bar had opened up nearby, so he went in for a break. He ordered a coffee and a hotdog.

The waitress brought him his food, the glistening fresh hotdog sausage peeking out between the two halves of the bun, along with some French mustard. Hanio couldn't help asking: "Are you free this evening?"

She was a thin, hard-looking girl. She wore heavy evening make-up even though it was still early in the day, and from the resolute line of her lips, she seemed determined not to smile ever in her life.

"It's still daytime."

"That's why I'm asking if you're free this evening."

"But I still don't know how the evening is going to pan out today."

"Oh, you mean you're a bit in the dark about the future?"

"That's right. We don't even know what's going to happen in fifteen minutes."

"That's going a bit far, isn't it—dividing everything up into such short spans of time?"

"Well, that's what they do on television. Every fifteen minutes, there are breaks for commercials. That way we get to look forward to what's coming next. That's how it works in real life too." She laughed out loud as she walked off. He had, in short, been given the cold shoulder.

But Hanio was not bothered. The girl clearly modeled her life on television. Not having to think too far ahead probably made everything certain, precise, and safe. And she could keep her options open. With a commercial break due to come on every fifteen minutes, why on earth should she commit herself to something arranged for so much later in the day?

There was nothing else to do but to return to his apartment, but Hanio drifted about from place to place, trying all the same to spend as little money as possible. It was night by the time he got back home.

The fifty thousand yen was tucked inside his breast pocket, but he could not help thinking he ought to hand back the money.

When would the old man appear next? Until he did turn up and they had settled accounts, he still had financial ownership of Hanio's life, so it was best to leave the "Sold" sign posted on his apartment door.

That night Hanio slept soundly. Next morning, he heard footsteps, which stopped outside his apartment. But whoever it was apparently saw the card because the footsteps then went away with no knock on the door. It might be a hit man, he suddenly thought. But no, that was unlikely. No need to think he was in some spurious thriller story. The water for his morning coffee came to the boil as he faced his reflection in the wall mirror. What a fool he was: he stuck out his tongue in a crude gesture.

The whole of the next day, Hanio was surprised how anxiously he awaited the old man. He wanted to meet him as soon as possible and get his life sorted out one way or another. A sale was a sale: the man surely ought to give a bit more attention to what he'd bought. It occurred to Hanio that the old fellow might turn up while he happened to be out, so he remained indoors the whole day.

The wintry sun went down. The concierge was in the habit of delivering the evening paper himself, and he slipped it under the door after dusk had settled.

Hanio opened the paper to an article on page three, and was startled to see a huge picture of Ruriko's face:

BEAUTY FOUND DROWNED IN SUMIDA RIVER

Suicide or murder, unclear. Name card "Ruriko Kishi" (address unknown) discovered in handbag left by side of bridge.

The article went on to paint the incident in lurid colors.

8

The news in the paper about Ruriko's death left Hanio dumbstruck. And at this very moment the old man chose to pay a visit.

He almost came tumbling into the apartment, such was his excitement. "You did it. Fantastic! Well done! And you got away without dying after all! Now that's what I call real business acumen. I'm so happy. So happy!" He cavorted around the room.

Irritated, Hanio grabbed him by the collar. "Get out of here, right now! I'm returning your fifty thousand, so just take it," he said, and thrust the money into the old man's pocket. "You used that money to buy my life. But I'm still alive, so I'm under no obligation to keep it."

"Hey, wait a minute. Not so fast. Why not tell me what happened before we decide on anything."

The old man dug his feet in and flapped his hands about in stiff resistance to being manhandled by Hanio. He grabbed hold of the inside door handle and rattled it about so loudly that Hanio feared that the other residents might emerge from their apartments. Finally prised away from the door handle, the old man sank to the floor, hissing through his teeth even more noisily than before. Crawling to a chair, he hoisted himself up on to it, his dignity restored at last.

"You shouldn't rough people up like that. Especially someone my age." Noticing the bills shoved into his pocket, he pulled them out angrily, and deposited them in a large cut-glass ashtray. Hanio watched with interest, half expecting the old man to set fire to them with a match. But he showed no sign of doing so. The crumpled bills began unfurling in the ashtray like the petals of some dirty artificial flower coming into bloom.

"Surely you can understand why I'm delighted? Even a youngster like you ought to be able to grasp how Ruriko made me suffer, how she treated me with utter contempt. That woman deserved her comeuppance. I assume you did sleep with her?"

Hanio felt his face flush, and he had to glance away.

"Bull's-eye, right? So you did get it on. Well? She's quite something, don't you think? Everyone hates her after they've shared her bed, because relations with all other women pale in comparison . . . I guess I should come clean and say that I'm actually too old now to get it up, even with her. And when a man gets that desperate about a woman, what other option is there but to finish her off?"

"That's a rather simplistic way of thinking about things. So, you're the one that killed her?"

"Hey, don't get funny with me. If I were capable of doing that myself, why come and ask you? No, the one who bumped her off—"

"So it was murder, plain and simple, was it?"

"What else could it be but murder?"

"For the life of me, I can't help clinging to the idea that it all came about by mistake, through a series of miscalculations. And for that reason I'm thinking of returning to that apartment tomorrow—"

"Don't even think of it. The police will be keeping a watch on the place, you can be sure. Do you seriously intend to let yourself get caught up in that? I really hope not."

"I guess you're right."

It wouldn't be worth it, Hanio knew. There was clearly little point in returning to the apartment now, especially since her body would no longer be there. But he was pretty sure that gun would still be chilling in the fridge.

"But, you know . . ." For the first time, Hanio loosened up and felt that he wanted to give the old man a detailed account of his experience.

The old man continued to make hissing sounds through his teeth as he listened, seemingly unaware that he was also betraying the lingering habits of his foppish youth. He played nervously with the knot of his tie and softly stroked what little hair he had left with hands that were spotted with age. He glanced out through the window, where his attention seemed to be drawn to a withered willow tree beneath the eaves of two adjoining houses: it caught the light reflected from the windows, and was bending in the cold night breeze. As he waited for Hanio to continue, the old man appeared lost in memories of his own bygone pleasures.

"I do find the fact that I wasn't killed amazing," Hanio went on. "Do you think there'd be a problem if I became a witness after the event?"

"Haven't you got it yet? That guy clearly came back with the express aim of killing Ruriko. You just happened to be in the way. Don't you see? Most likely she'd drained him of every ounce of physical energy until he couldn't take it anymore. If he'd killed you both there and then, he would have been sending you off together, and losing her to another man for good. That's why he deliberately made a point of killing her alone, in a way that would keep her all to himself. Of course, what he saw you both up to would no doubt have hardened his resolve."

"But is he really the murderer? He just didn't look the type."

"How blind can you be? That guy is a mobster and a notorious gangland boss. Even if you did become a witness, he'd find some way of wriggling out of the clutches of the law. Right at this moment, he's most probably putting on some brazen display in that very apartment, crying and yelling over Ruriko's death. It hardly needs me to tell you, murder cases always soon get forgotten. So it's best that the matter remains unsolved. But I appreciate that you threw yourself into your work without poking your nose into things that don't concern you . . . Here, let me give you another fifty thousand as a little celebratory bonus."

The old man tossed another five ten-thousand-yen notes into the ashtray, and prepared to go home.

"Well, I suppose this is the last we will see of each other," said Hanio.

"I hope so. I don't suppose Ruriko mentioned me at all?"

Hanio could not resist a teasing reply. "Well, she did and she didn't."

"What?" The old man turned pale. "Don't tell me she let on about my personal details."

"Mmm, I'm not sure about that."

"Are you trying to blackmail me?"

"Even if I were, it's not as if you are guilty of any crime in law, right?"

"That's true . . ."

"All you and I did was to try and turn the gears of this perilous world a tiny bit. Normally such a minor thing would have had no effect at all. But no sooner had I decided it was worth throwing my life away for it than a murder scene materialized, seemingly out of thin air. That's amazing, wouldn't you say?"

"You're a weird one. You have as much heart as a vending machine."

"That's right. Stick a coin in me, and you get out what you paid for. It's all or nothing when it comes to machines."

"Can a human really behave so like a robot?"

"Quite a revelation, isn't it?"

Hanio's broad grin was met with a horrified look. "So how much do you want?"

"If I want anything, I'll get in touch. But I don't need any more money from you today."

The old man escaped through the door to make his getaway.

Hanio called after him. "And you can forget about the Siamese cat. After all, I'm alive."

Reaching round the door, he turned the card back to the side that read "Life for Sale." Then he retreated inside with a yawn.

9

He was a man who had already died once.

There was no reason why he should feel any sense of responsibility or attachment to the world. To him, it was nothing more than a sheet of newspaper covered in the scribblings of cockroaches. So how did Ruriko fit in?

Ruriko's body had been discovered. The police must be running around looking for the culprit. No one had caught sight of him in Villa Borghese, of that he was sure, and he hadn't met anyone during the twenty minutes he waited in the corridor. When he left the building, no one seemed to be tailing him back to his apartment. In short, he had slipped back into the world with all the commotion of a wisp of smoke. Why would he be summoned as a potential suspect? The only uncertain part was if the old man got hauled in by the police and mentioned his name. But this was really not worth worrying about. After all, the old man was clearly wary of having anything to do with Hanio.

So even if Hanio had been the murderer, the case would very likely run into the ground.

At this point in his thoughts, Hanio shuddered. Could he be sure that he wasn't the murderer?

Considering how bizarre the whole episode had been, what if he had unconsciously fallen victim to the hypnotic powers of that strange man in the beret, and had ended up doing away with Ruriko? Maybe he'd done it during the night when he was in a deep sleep.

Could his decision to put his life up for sale be linked to the murder?

No, that was a crazy idea. It had nothing to do with him. Nothing at all. He'd cut all his ties with human society long ago, hadn't he?

But if that were true, what to make of these sweet memories of Ruriko that returned to him again and again? What did it mean that he had experienced such intense physical pleasure with her? Had the woman named Ruriko actually ever existed?

He was determined not to worry about his part in it all. It would only make him ill.

How could he entertain himself this evening? A man who had managed to sell his life for one hundred thousand yen once would surely be able to sell it again.

Hanio was in no mood to do anything as mundane as having a drink. On a sudden impulse, he took out a stuffed toy mouse with a funny face from the cupboard. Some time ago, a girl who made this kind of handicraft had presented it to him as a gift.

The mouse had a pointed snout, like a fox, with a few wispy hairs at the tip of its nose. It was a rather commonplace design, with tiny eyes made from black beads. One curious feature was that the mouse was clad in a lunatic's straitjacket: a strong white sheet bound both his paws together tightly against his chest so that they couldn't budge an inch. On the front of the jacket were some words written in English: "Beware: patient prone to violence."

Hanio put the mouse's inertness down entirely to the straitjacket. Taking his reasoning to its logical conclusion, he decided that the very ordinariness and nondescript nature of its mousy face was actually proof of its lunacy.

"Right then, Mousikins." His words elicited no response. Maybe the mouse had a misanthropic streak.

This was not exactly the moment to dwell on the difference between country and city rodents, but he had the feeling this was a mouse from the sticks that had been tricked by some sly Tokyo cousin into changing its abode and had ended up getting crushed under the huge pressure of life in the big city. Worn down by its meaningless solitary existence, it had ended up developing a propensity to violence.

Hanio decided to share a leisurely evening meal with it. He sat the mouse on the opposite side of the table, tucked a napkin into the top of its straitjacket, and left it there while he prepared the meal. The demented mouse sat bolt upright as it waited.

After giving some thought to what he might serve the mouse,

Hanio prepared bits of cheese and small pieces of steak that it could nibble easily with its sharp teeth. He also made a portion for himself and sat down.

"OK, Mousikins. Grub's up. Don't stand on ceremony."

Despite his encouragement, there was no reply. Apparently the demented mouse also suffered from an eating disorder.

"Hey, why no eating? After all the effort I put into the cooking, don't you like it?"

Sure enough, no reply.

"Maybe you need some music playing while you eat. You like your luxuries, don't you? Let me put on a quiet piece that might be to your taste."

He got up from the table and put Debussy's "La Cathédrale engloutie" on the stereo. The mouse remained sullen and tight-lipped.

"You're an odd one. You're a mouse, so you should be able to eat without using your paws."

No reply. Hanio suddenly flew into a rage. "So you don't like my cooking? Right then, this is what you get." He knocked over the small plate of steak and shoved the mouse's face into the food. The shock sent the mouse tipping back effortlessly over his chair onto the floor.

Hanio picked the mouse up in his fingers. "What's this? Are you dead? Doesn't take much to kill you. You're pathetic. Well? What have you got to say for yourself? Don't expect a proper funeral. I doubt you're even worth a single night's wake. You're just a mouse, an ordinary little mouse. Why don't you simply shrivel up into a husk in some filthy hole. You were absolutely worthless while you were alive. You're equally worthless now you're dead." Picking up the dead mouse, he threw it back into the cupboard.

He sampled the tiny slices of steak left by the mouse. They tasted delicious, like meaty sweets.

Hanio thought things through, listening to Debussy's "Submerged Cathedral." A bystander might have seen this as a pathetic game played by a lonely person desperate to be rescued from his loneliness. But how sad it would be to see loneliness as an enemy! It was his unconditional ally. No doubt about it.

At that moment, there was a stealthy knock on the door.

10

He opened it to find an utterly nondescript middle-aged woman, her hair pulled back in a bun.

"I've come in response to your newspaper ad."

"I see. Please come in. I'm in the middle of eating, but I'll be finished soon."

"Sorry to trouble you." The woman stepped in gingerly, looking around as she did so.

Was there any endeavour more worthy than to purchase a person's life? So why did all the clients who came to his place look so furtive?

As he ate, Hanio stole glances in the woman's direction. From the inelegant way she wore her kimono he sensed she was no ordinary housewife: more like an elderly spinster, perhaps, someone who taught English literature at a girls' college of higher education. She would have nothing but vivacious young students in her care, and the fact that they were all the same sex would make her even more determined to stand out by positively letting herself go to seed. It's often the case that such women are much younger than they appear.

"To tell the truth, every day I've been making my way surreptitiously to your front door. But you've had that card up saying 'Sold' all the time, as you know. What does that word mean? If that were the real state of affairs, it would mean you were dead. Even today I had more or less resigned myself to the fact that it would be hopeless, but I still came. I was so relieved to see the card turned over to the side with 'Life for Sale' written on it."

"Yes, I managed to complete the job I was assigned. I sold my life but, as you see, I am still alive."

Hanio brought in two cups of coffee from the kitchenette, one for the woman.

"So why have you come to see me?"

"It's a little embarrassing for me to tell you."

"You have nothing to worry about, believe me."

"You can say that. But it's embarrassing, nevertheless."

After a short pause, the woman discarded all reticence and looked directly at Hanio. "If you sell me your life, this time you probably won't be able to return home alive. Are you happy with that?"

II

When Hanio failed to turn a hair, the woman looked deflated. Sipping the coffee with puckered lips, she repeated her warning, but this time with an edge in her voice. "I mean it. So you're all right with that, are you?"

"Yes, I am. So, what do you want from me?"

"Let me explain."

The woman self-consciously drew the edges of her kimono together over her lap, as if fearful she might be assaulted in this room alone with a man, though, for Hanio's part, nothing about her invited any interest.

"Now, my job involves lending books out in a small library.

There's no point you asking me which one. After all, there are as many libraries in Tokyo as there are police stations. Anyway, as a single woman with time on my hands, I like to buy various evening newspapers on the way home from work. Once I'm home, I immerse myself in reading the advice columns, classified ads, job vacancies, exchange columns, and the like. At first I was an avid member of a pen-pal club, and I even went so far as to set up a mailbox address in order to exchange letters. But I was aware that meeting anyone in the flesh would end in disaster, so I just led them on a bit and then abruptly cut the correspondence."

"What do you mean, meeting anyone would end in disaster?" Hanio's question was cruel.

"Everybody has their own fantasies," the woman replied irritably, avoiding his eyes. "You shouldn't try to humiliate people like that. I'm in the middle of telling you my story. In any case, the pen-pal thing bored me after a bit, and I began to seek out other ways of keeping myself entertained. But they were very hard to come by."

"That's exactly why I put out my 'Life for Sale' ad."

"Must you interrupt? Let me finish my story! Around February this year—ten months ago, I guess—I happened to catch sight of a notice in one of the newspapers: 'Looking to buy *The Illustrated Book of Japanese Beetles*, published 1927, by Gentarō Yamawaki. Will pay two hundred thousand yen. Must be an unabridged edition. Contact: mailbox 2778, Central Post Office.'

"Now that is not a bad price at all to be offering. The market in secondhand books seems to have taken off in recent years, and the price must have meant it was a rare volume. The person who had posted the notice had probably made inquiries at secondhand bookshops with no success, and then decided to advertise in the newspaper. My instinct was right, it turns out. It seems I have a pretty good nose for business.

"Now, at the end of each fiscal year, a major tidy-up takes place in my library. We take out all the volumes in the stacks, give them a good dusting and put them back in the correct order. It's quite a job. Among several hundred volumes of which half are hidden away under the natural science classification I noticed last year that there were as many as ten books on entomology. In the fields of medicine and physics, recent inventions and discoveries leading to new drugs and other treatments mean that certain books become totally redundant. But not so in entomology, as I was well aware. Brushing away the dust, I opened up each volume and peeped inside.

"And then I came across the volume by Gentarō Yamawaki entitled *The Illustrated Book of Japanese Beetles* and published by Yūendō in 1927. I immediately recalled the newspaper notice I'd seen about the book, and an evil thought—the first such thought during my long years at the library—took root."

12

Everything the woman went on to say indicated that, until that moment, she had lived a perfectly crime-free life. But, while her fantasies had until then remained half-baked, the prospect of two hundred thousand yen in cash meant that somewhere deep in her heart there had suddenly crackled into life a desire for clothes and luxury goods that would allow her to look other women in the eye.

Before she knew it she had concealed *The Illustrated Book of Japanese Beetles* in a piece of waste paper she happened to have at hand. She continued with the reorganization as if nothing was amiss.

Then, telling her colleague she was going to throw something away, she left the room with the waste paper, the book hidden inside. She secretly took out the book and concealed it in a friend's room for the time being. Her plan was that, even if this book stamped with the library mark happened to turn up somewhere in the future, she had the ready-made alibi that she had accidentally thrown it away with the waste paper.

Anyway, that evening back at her apartment, she opened the book, her heart racing, as if she were opening some scandalous publication. The smell of dust arose from between the pages.

As she had suspected, it was the kind of rare book that curiosity seekers would relish. It was hard to tell whether it had been written for pure pleasure or as a work of art in its own right. Considering how old the printing was, the tricolor illustrations were extremely beautiful. There were dazzling images of beetles in their various stages, showing the different markings on their backs, like a color advertisement for fashion accessories. In each illustration, the beetle had a number and a scientific name, as well as a description of its appearance and habitat.

But it was the chapter titles that struck her as most curious. They did not conform to any scientific system of classification she had seen before. The table of contents was as follows:

Type 1: Sensual Genus (Aphrodisiac Order,
Stimulatory Order)
Type 2: Soporific Genus
Type 3: Homicidal Genus

Inevitably, as a spinster, she felt obliged to skip the first chapter entirely—though of course she was dying to read it—and gave her undivided attention to the two that followed.

Some unknown person, she noted, had covered the third chapter, "Type 3: Homicidal Genus," with a mass of untidy red circles and lines.

One section that stood out was "Variety of Scarab Beetle

(*Anthypna pectinata*)" on page 132. The illustration showed a rather ordinary-looking small brown beetle with almost no neck linking its head and thorax. A pair of antlers grew out of its armored head, which was also covered in brush-like protrusions. The insect looked vaguely familiar. The description was as follows:

> Native to Tokyo Region, Honshu. Found around rose, harlequin glorybower (*Clerodendrum trichotomum*) and a great variety of other flowers.
>
> A relatively easy beetle to come by, its soporific properties are surprisingly little known. Even less well known is the fact that it can be used to potentially lethal effect: homicide under the guise of suicide. This is done by drying the beetle and grinding it into a powder, then mixing it with the hypnotic sedative bromovalerylurea. Once administered to the recipient, this potion allows for the conveyance of commands to the brain while the person is asleep, and facilitates a wide range of suicidal methods.

Here the description ended.

But this was all she needed to see into the criminal intentions of the person who had placed the notice in the newspaper in search of the book. With a razor blade she scraped away the library ownership stamp on the book's inside cover and title page. She then wrote a message out on a postcard, which she addressed to the mailbox number given at the bottom of the notice, and posted it: "I have unabridged edition in my possession. If still required, can supply according to stipulated conditions for immediate payment on delivery. Please advise appropriate time and place. Sundays best if possible." To this she appended her own mailbox number.

Just four days later, a reply arrived. The date specified in the letter was the following Sunday, which was fine for her. But the location was a bit of a walk from Fujisawa Station in Chigasaki. A map was enclosed showing the address of a house that was evidently a holiday villa belonging to a family named Nakajima.

Only one thing gave her pause. Quite a few of the characters in the letter were written incorrectly, in a strangely childish hand. There was even a mistake in her name. "Something doesn't seem quite right," she thought.

That Sunday, on a bright, sunny spring afternoon, and with a cold breeze blowing, she walked from Fujisawa Station in the direction of the sea, following the directions given on the map.

She left the main road and turned off into a side street. The tarmac immediately gave way to an unpaved sandy track. The stone walls of rows of holiday villas were almost completely obscured by sand dunes. Yellow butterflies fluttered here and there. There was not a single sign of human activity. Of course these days lots of commuters who work in Tokyo have houses in places like this. But this little spot seemed every inch the long-standing holiday-home enclave, and it was deathly silent.

She passed through an old gate that bore the "Nakajima" nameplate to find a long sandy path leading to the house. A Western-style home surrounded by pines came into view. The large garden was in an unkempt state and the damp sea wind blew hard and strong through it.

She pressed the bell. To her surprise a fat ruddy-faced foreigner wearing a loud plaid sports jacket came to the door. The foreigner's level of Japanese was excellent—to such a degree that it rather unsettled her.

"Thank you for your letter. We've been waiting for you to visit. Please, come on through."

He led her into a room where there was another foreigner, this one as skinny as a stick insect. He got up from his chair and greeted her courteously.

She had come fully prepared to make her escape if things

got nasty. The set of heavy American-style rattan chairs placed directly on the tatami mats of this large, uncarpeted room strongly suggested that this was a temporary residence. There was no other furniture of note, though a color TV had been placed in the alcove traditionally used for ornaments. It was not switched on, and the television screen brought to mind the bluish-black surface gleam of a swamp.

The paper sliding doors had been left open, and along one side of the corridor, its floor all sandy, were some ill-fitting glass doors that rattled endlessly in the wind. She noticed they were unlocked, and felt confident she could get away through any number of open doors.

The thin man offered her alcohol, which she declined, so a glass of lemonade was placed before her instead. The thought that they might slip her a sleeping potion before their business was concluded so worried her that she did not touch it despite being parched.

The fat foreigner who was fluent in Japanese offered her a chair, but he said nothing further. No mention was made of the illustrated beetle book. She placed on her lap the shopping bag that held it and patted it ostentatiously.

Still no response.

The two men continued to whisper in English, ignoring her. She did not understand a word of what they were saying but, judging from their expressions, they seemed to be discussing something serious. Her impatience grew.

Just then, the doorbell rang.

"Oh, maybe, Henry . . ." The fat foreigner had suddenly switched to English as he hurried to the door.

An elderly foreign man, quite dapper, dressed for the outdoors, entered, preceded by a dachshund with lank ears, its fur oily-looking, rather like a seal. From the attitude of the other two men, it was clear that this man was their boss. The pair introduced him to her in a very deferential manner. She was not at all pleased when the dog proceeded to give itself a good shake.

The man appeared to speak no Japanese, and offered a few quick pleasantries in English. The fat foreigner acted as interpreter.

"Henry expresses his thanks that you kindly came as agreed, and he offers you his deepest respects."

That's going a bit far, she thought to herself. But he continued: "I see you brought the book."

Finally, he had broached it. She felt relieved. She took the book out of the bag. "The money, please, the *mo-nee*. Don't forget."

She had expected the fat foreigner to interpret, but this was ignored. The thought that they might get something out of her for nothing caused her throat to tighten.

The elderly foreigner flicked through the book's pages numerous times. The glow on his face indicated satisfaction.

"What a relief!" said the fat man. "All the copies of this book we've obtained so far have only been about thirty pages long, with whole sections missing. You will know that the Japanese police used to censor passages in books at the time that this was published. This is the first unabridged version we have seen and, as you can observe, Henry is delighted. He was checking it through before he paid you the cash . . . Here is the two hundred thousand yen. Go ahead, please confirm the amount."

Dimples formed in the fat man's cheeks, shiny white like enamel, as he handed over the money. The dog came up to sniff the bills.

She was relieved to count out twenty crisp ten-thousand-yen bills and, seeing no reason to stay any longer, rose from her chair with the intention of taking her leave there and then.

"Oh, so you're leaving?" the fat man said. The thin man also stood up to bar her way.

"Since you've been so kind as to come all this way, won't you at least share something to eat before you depart?"

"I'd rather not."

Now that she was about to take her leave, she felt she didn't have to mince words. She could see herself getting into some frightening scenario otherwise.

The fat man suddenly lent over and whispered in her ear: "What about another five hundred thousand?"

"Eh?" She stood there wondering if she'd heard correctly.

13

Hanio's curiosity was piqued. Nothing about this woman drew him to her as a member of the opposite sex, but her tale thoroughly engrossed him.

"Hey, that is quite an adventure. So did you manage to come away with that extra money?"

"The money didn't interest me. I managed somehow to slip out of their clutches and make my way home. Though no one seemed actually to be tailing me, I ran so fast I was soaked through with perspiration by the time I arrived at the station."

"And did you ever go back?"

"Well, actually . . ."

"So you did receive another call?"

"No, I was just intrigued to know what had happened next, so one Sunday in July when the weather was sunny and I had some time on my hands, I went back to check. There was clearly someone in, so I rang the bell, but this time a Japanese housewife came to the door. I was surprised and asked what had happened to Henry. She told me she'd rented the place to a foreigner for a brief two or three weeks in the spring, but she had no idea of what had become of him afterward. She was quite unfriendly, so I came straight back home."

"Well, this is all very interesting, but what has it got to do with me?"

"I'm just getting to that part."

She bummed a cigarette off him and lit it. There was nothing flirtatious in her action. In fact, she was like an old woman in a lottery booth who persuades someone to buy one of her tickets and then has the effrontery to ask that same customer for a smoke.

"After that, I didn't hear a thing. I kept my mailbox as before, but no one contacted me. And then I saw your 'Life for Sale' ad, and that set me thinking. It occurred to me that the five hundred thousand yen might very well have been an inducement for me to act as their guinea pig in an experiment. It made a lot of sense. I thought then that if they saw your ad, they would be certain to communicate with you."

"But I've had no such contact. And anyway, don't you think foreign crooks would have taken themselves straight off to Hong Kong or Singapore?"

"Only if they were in the ACS," she said.

"What?" Hanio was dumbfounded.

14

So this woman knew about the ACS too!

That Asian mobster had described the ACS as a mere fiction, the stuff of thriller mangas, but Hanio started to wonder whether the organization was in fact real and had something to do with Ruriko's death. Having heard what the woman in front of him had to say, he now felt that everything was being woven together into a single tapestry. Hanio started to suspect that his willingness to sell his own life had turned him into an ACS pawn.

But there was no way this woman was part of the ACS.

Surely no one who was affiliated with such a masterly organization would mention it so carelessly. She had simply given an honest report of her meeting with the foreigners in Chigasaki—there was nothing more to it than that.

"So what is the ACS?" he asked.

"You mean you don't know? The Asia Confidential Service is a secret organization said to be involved in narcotic drugs smuggling."

"How do you know about it?"

"A foreigner who turned out to be a drug dealer used to be a visitor to the library. He came in every day, and we thought to ourselves, 'Wow, he studies hard!' But he was also sociable and handsome—I heard it said that he was an assistant professor at C— University in Los Angeles. Every day he seemed to come in to do his research, into Japanese history, so we all assumed he was a renowned specialist in his field.

"Pretty soon, I started to notice that a Japanese man, clearly unemployed, had become a frequent occupant of the seat next to the foreigner. The two of them seemed to strike up quite a friendship, and the Japanese man began to borrow book after book, all on the subject of Japanese history. It got to a point where a young female colleague of mine remarked to me: 'What a funny state of affairs! He's Japanese, and yet he's being taught about Japanese history by that foreigner, who clearly has a much deeper knowledge than he does.'

"It wasn't long before the foreigner became friendly with the girl at the reception desk, and the subject came up of going out to a nearby coffee shop. But unfortunately for the girl, the foreigner seemed keen to observe propriety and he insisted that she choose another friend to accompany them. The girl was pretty miffed when he asked us both out. I wasn't particularly bothered, but I went along for the meal.

"It must have been May last year. I remember the evening

vividly. The library had just closed and the bright afternoon sunshine was all around us as we walked along the avenue of beautiful trees that leads from the library to the main road. We decided to take him to one of our regular coffee shops, and all three of us felt buoyed up by a mixture of pleasure and competitiveness.

"So we sat down and started a conversation about various things. Of course, his Japanese was quite good, and he certainly had the gift of the gab.

" 'Sitting here with two beauties, drinking this foreign-made tea, which after all was imported into Japan by early European traders, I feel just like a Tokugawa shogun must have felt, sitting with his harem of ladies in the inner sanctum of Edo Castle.'

"We all laughed merrily. If you took it the wrong way, it might have seemed rather crude, but coming from Mr. Dodwell—that was his name—well, it was charming. His Japanese wasn't perfect, if anything rather lacking in finesse, and there was something about him that was a bit too glib—he reminded me of a machine that is rather too well oiled. In the course of our conversation, I remember, he suddenly paused and then asked, quite amiably: 'I wonder, have either of you heard of the ACS?'

" 'Is it the name of a TV station? Mmm, I haven't heard of any such channel in Japan. Perhaps an American TV station?' my friend asked. 'Or maybe the name of a company that makes TVs? I'd say it was an international agricultural cooperative organization. "Agriculture Cooperative System," something like that.'

"She was just showing off what little education she had, so I glared right at her.

"He listened, smiling broadly. 'You're getting warmer with that last answer. It does appear to be an international organization. A secret one, by the name of the Asia Confidential Service. It's a little scary, actually. And it's closer than you'd think.'

"We listened to him intently, slightly disturbed now.

"Mr. Dodwell continued: 'You've seen the Japanese guy who

sits next to me in the library all the time, asking me questions about history? You rarely get that kind of pest in a library, and I've found it a real pain. To top it all, his questions have all been utterly inane. One day he asked me, completely out of the blue: "How many children did the fourteenth-century samurai Masashige Kusunoki have?" I hadn't the foggiest, so I just pretended I knew the answer and told him ten—whereupon his face suddenly lit up. Knowing what I know now, I'm pretty sure that my reply may just happen to have been the correct reply to some sort of secret password.

" 'Even then, he didn't come clean, and he didn't let down his guard. But the day before yesterday, he suddenly informed me he had decided that I wasn't a member of the ACS after all. I didn't know what he was on about. I asked what the ACS was. He looked a bit smug when he replied: "Asia Confidential Service . . . I'm so relieved. I mistook you for someone else, and came within an inch of killing you." And then he took his leave. The thought that I almost got it in the neck scared the living daylights out of me. To think I'd been under suspicion of being a member of the organization!'

" 'Wow, that's scary. You should have informed the police immediately,' we both chimed in.

" 'Well, sometimes stirring the pot can cause even more trouble.' Mr. Dodwell spoke with a quiet tension in his voice.

"Mr. Dodwell never came to the library again. But I never forgot the name 'ACS.' "

15

At this point, Hanio broke in. "So maybe Dodwell, if that was his real name, actually was the ACS member."

"But if that was the case, why would he come out and mention it?" asked the woman.

"Maybe he thought his cover in the library was blown, and he was trying to get a handle on the situation by sounding you out."

"Who knows?" The woman was thinking about something else.

"OK, to return to the main issue."

"Yes. The reason I came to buy your life. Seeing as you still haven't heard anything from that foreigner Henry whom I met previously, we can assume that the offer of five hundred thousand, the one he made to me that time I was about to leave, still stands.

"The moment I saw your ad, I knew you were the right person to test that scarab beetle drug on. A referral fee of one hundred thousand yen is all I need for myself. So could I interest you in selling me your life for a fee of four hundred thousand? I would assume responsibility for sending that whole amount to your next of kin, and, to put your mind at rest, I would do it before your death. Does that sound like a deal?"

"I don't have any next of kin."

"In which case, what should I do with the money?"

"Why don't you use it to buy some large animal—a crocodile, a gorilla, something like that—to lavish your attention on? Probably the best thing for you would be to give up on marriage completely and spend the rest of your life with whichever of those animals you choose. I don't believe any other partner would make you happier. But don't even think of making handbags out of it. All you have to do is feed the creature every day, exercise it, and put your heart and soul into raising it. And each time you look into its eyes you'll be reminded of me."

"You're a very odd person."

"No, you're the odd one."

16

The woman drafted a letter to Henry, which she sent to his mailbox address via special delivery. Her message was brief: "Will take part in pharmaceutical test for five hundred thousand yen. Have my own subject." The response was immediate, with a designated date and location for the test: January the third in the Shibaura warehouse district of Tokyo.

Hanio and the woman arranged to meet beforehand, and together they made their way to the deserted district under a cold sliver of moon that looked as if it was being tossed about by the wind in the wintry night. They knocked on the designated door. On the fifth knock it swung open. They followed a staircase down through numerous twists and turns to a cold metal door.

As they pushed it open, a blast of thick warm air hit them in the face. They entered a well-heated, Western-style room, quite large and laid with a red carpet.

Two large square windows, set side by side, gave onto a polluted seabed scene. Not a single fish swam in the water, which was filled with all kinds of accumulated debris and other odds and ends. Close to one window floated what might have been the small whitish corpse of a fish, but it looked more like a human fetus and Hanio hurriedly averted his eyes.

The room itself was comfortably set out: red electric lighting gave the impression of artificial logs flickering in the fireplace. An electric fire no doubt avoided the need for a vent.

Three foreigners were there, waiting for them. The ageing foreigner with a dachshund on a lead had to be Henry.

The woman was the first to break the ice. "You remember you asked me whether I needed five hundred thousand yen."

"Yes," one of the two younger foreigners replied in Japanese.

"I assumed you were asking if I was willing to become a guinea pig for the drug."

"Your assumption was correct."

"I've brought this man along to be the guinea pig for me. I've already bought his life from him, so give me the five hundred thousand now, if you please."

This caught the foreigner off guard, and he addressed Henry in English. A whispered discussion between the three men ensued.

"So, are you really content with the possibility that you may die?" said the first foreigner.

"Yes," Hanio replied calmly. "And what are you looking so astonished for? You all know, I'm sure, that human life is quite meaningless, and people are just puppets anyway. What's the big deal?"

"You have just the right attitude. Ever since we got hold of that book, we've collected as many scarab beetles as we could lay our hands on, mixing them with bromovalerylurea to make the drug. We've tried it out on a couple of subjects and, as it says in the book, they become susceptible to our instructions. But we haven't yet got to the point of persuading someone to commit suicide. So we're still not sure whether the instinct for life will stop someone going through with it when the crunch comes. But now that we have someone like you who's willing to die, we can finally carry out the test."

"Well, hand over the five hundred thousand first," repeated the woman.

Henry instructed one of the men to bring him a stash of banknotes. He carefully counted out fifty ten-thousand-yen bills and handed the cash over to the librarian. The woman removed ten of the bills, putting them in her handbag, and gave the rest to Hanio.

A pistol lay on top of a table nearby.

"It's loaded. The safety catch is off. If you point it toward you and pull the trigger, it's game over," one of the men said.

Hanio sat down in an armchair next to the table and swallowed the powdered drug that was handed him, washing it down with some water . . .

Nothing unusual was happening. He had no premonition of how drastically his whole world was going to change.

The powdered remains of some lazy, good-for-nothing beetle, whose only mission in its unremarkable life was to fly from flower to flower, sticking its dirty little nose deep into pollen until it choked, had now entered his body. But this offered no clue to the manner in which his world was about to turn into a flower garden.

The old spinster's hard face suddenly loomed up in front of him. He got an eyeful of every detail—every wrinkle beneath her eyes, every pore on the rough skin of her cheeks, every loose strand of her hair. All of it calling out like an urgent clangor of bells: "I love you . . . I love you . . . I love you . . ."

The words were deafeningly loud. Hanio wanted to cover his ears.

Once the world has been transformed into something meaningful, some feel they can die without regret. Others feel that they exist in a world without meaning, so what's the point of living? But where do these two sets of feelings converge? For Hanio, both paths led to the same thing: death.

Before long, his surroundings turned viscous and began to gyrate. He watched as the wallpaper bulged, billowing out as if blown by the wind. Flocks of what looked like yellow birds fluttered around him. They made him dizzy.

The sound of music reached him from somewhere. This music evoked the vision of a green forest swaying like seaweed, which then changed into flowers—they looked like wisteria—drooping from branch after branch with countless wild horses galloping in circles below. He was not sure why this particular fantasy should have arisen, but he sensed that his everyday world—the world of those newspapers filled with cockroach-shaped letters—was doing its very best to transform itself into something marvelous. But maybe "doing its best" was a little over the top, Hanio reflected: A meaningless world doing its best? What a pathetic idea!

He did not feel nauseous, but neither did he seem to be in a trance. Suddenly, his surroundings underwent another transformation. Numerous gigantic needles sprang up around his body. These needles glittered in the light, and then, cactus-like, flowers unfolded from the needle points. The flowers were red and yellow and white. To Hanio's eyes, the blossoms appeared tawdry. The needles then turned into television antennae, and he watched as green plastic wastebaskets floated in the air inside the room, filling the entire space as if they were giant advertising blimps.

"It's all so banal. The whole world is a waste of time." Hanio was not impressed.

"How are you feeling? Do you think you could die now?" A voice reached him.

"Absolutely."

His body suddenly appeared to be floating. Until then he had felt bound to the chair, but now his limbs seemed free to move. Yet he was surprised what a carefree thrill he experienced whenever he moved his limbs in accordance with someone else's instructions. He never imagined it would be like this.

"All right, let's go with it. Follow my instructions. I'll take it nice and slow."

"Thank you."

"Stretch your right hand out."

"Like this?"

"Like that. Exactly."

This was all going on inside Hanio's own head, so his words ought to have been inaudible even to himself. Yet there the other man was, giving instructions in response to what Hanio said.

"Now, you should be able to reach the hard black object on top of the table with your fingers. Take it firmly in your grasp. There we go. Don't touch the trigger yet. Now, bring it gently up to your head. Easy now, easy. Relax your shoulders. Better? Press the muzzle against your temple. It probably feels a bit cold. Rather nice, yes? Gives you a fresh feeling, doesn't it? A feeling of relief, just like one of those cooling pads for your forehead when you have a fever. Now, nice and gently, place your forefinger on the trigger . . ."

17

Hanio held the gun muzzle to his temple, finger on trigger.

At that moment, he was aware that someone had lunged toward him, the gun was snatched away, and there was an almighty bang right next to him. A dog began to yelp, an incessant clamor that resounded painfully in his ears.

The shock seemed to break the drug's effect. Giving his head a shake, he rose to his feet. Everything in the room came into remarkably sharp focus. The woman was slumped in a twisted heap at his feet, blood pouring from her forehead.

The fat man with the ruddy face, the man who looked like a skinny stick insect, Henry the elegant gentleman: all three stood, stunned, over her corpse.

Holding a hand to his groggy head, Hanio craned his neck to get a good look at her dead body. The woman held the gun in her right hand.

"What happened?" Hanio asked the florid foreigner.

"She died," the man answered vacantly, breaking his silence in Japanese.

"Why?"

"She must have loved you. Must have loved you to bits. That's the only logical explanation, isn't it? And so she chose to die in your place. But if the thought of watching you die was so unbearable to her, why not just take the gun out of your hand? Why did she have to kill herself?"

Hanio's thoughts were all over the place, but he did his best to remain focused. It was obvious why she had killed herself. She had become infatuated with him but, not believing that she would be loved in return, she took her own life. There could be no other explanation.

"It's suicide, no question about it," the foreigner continued. "We don't have anything to worry about."

The thought of how they were going to sort things out afterward was the last thing Hanio had been thinking about.

So she had taken a shine to him: what a tiresome thought! Even more tiresome was that she had to be such an ugly woman, who had then chosen to do away with herself. Extraordinary! There were no two ways about it. Both times he had tried selling his life to others, but it was they who had come to a sticky end.

Hanio watched the foreigners coolly, wondering what course they would choose. Perhaps they might finish him off there and then.

The three of them huddled together, conversing in whispers, while the dachshund continued to growl at the dead body. The sight of blood seemed to have stirred up something savage in this otherwise overly domesticated creature.

The blood oozed stealthily from under the corpse onto the surrounding floor, as if using the confusion of the moment to make its escape. The woman's gaping mouth appeared as a dark cavity that presented a secret route to the end of the world.

Her eyes were slightly open, with a straggle of hair caught across one of them.

"Come to think of it, this is the first time I've ever got a good view of a dead person," said Hanio to himself. "I never saw even my mother and father's bodies up this close. A dead body reminds me a bit of a bottle of whisky. If you drop the bottle and it cracks, what's inside pours out. It's only natural."

The leaden sea moved restlessly on the other side of the windows. The foreigners were still deep in conversation. Hanio had a poor grasp of English, but his ears caught words to do with flight numbers, airlines, and airplanes. One of the men took the ten-thousand-yen bills from the woman's handbag, wrapping his hand in a handkerchief before doing so. He pressed the money into Hanio's hand, saying: "Here's some hush money. If you blab a word . . ." He made a cutting sign across his throat, and uttered a sound that curdled the blood.

They took him to their car and dropped him off at Hamamatsuchō Station. All three remained silent, as if wilfully ignoring him.

As the car drove off, Hanio gave a brief wave and immediately turned his back. He could have been taking leave of a few friends after a picnic.

After purchasing a train ticket, he made his way up the stairs. His head began to play tricks on him again: the dreary concrete steps seemed to go on forever. He tried to concentrate hard on climbing them, but however far he went he never seemed to reach the platform. As he continued, the steps seemed to increase in number. He was aware that somewhere up above him could be heard the shrill sound of guards' whistles, departing trains, and large crowds alighting, but it all seemed a long way away from the steps he was climbing.

He thought of himself as already dead. Morality, emotions, everything—all meaningless. He was completely free. And yet his mind remained weighed down with the love of that woman who had just died. Weren't other people supposed to be nothing more than cockroaches to him?

Just when the steps began to resemble an interminable waterfall gushing down over him, he suddenly emerged onto the station platform. A train had arrived. Hanio boarded, thoroughly exhausted. Inside the carriage, it was preternaturally bright and completely deserted. The plastic-laminated hanging straps swayed uniformly in the air. He took hold of one. Actually, it was more accurate to say that a white strap took hold of him.

18

Back at the apartment, he waited anxiously to see how things would play out. Feeling exhausted, he flipped the card on his door to read "Sold." How strange that his exhaustion meant there would have to be a stay of execution! Even flirting with the notion of death seemed to require energy.

No article appeared in the newspaper, either the next day or the day after that, regarding the discovery of the body of a woman who had committed suicide in some strange, undersea den. No doubt her corpse was still there, rotting away.

Gradually, Hanio's everyday feelings returned to him, the very same feelings he had experienced since his botched suicide: that everything was unreal and dishonest. The world he inhabited lacked all sadness or joy, nothing was clearly defined in it. A kind of meaninglessness infused his life both day and night, like the soft glow from indirect light.

"That woman. She didn't exist. That secret underwater room. All that crazy stuff never happened." This is what he decided to believe.

Having put his mind at rest, he decided to go into town. The festivities for the New Year were still going on. It felt odd not to have embraced a woman for such a long time.

As he walked through Shinjuku, his attention was caught by the backside of a girl entering a shop where a sale was on. It was warm, but the fact that she wore no coat set her apart even so. Covered by a slightly faded green plaid skirt, her bottom in the winter sunlight seemed crammed with the very essence of life, as voluptuous as any painted by Renoir. She exuded the kind of glossy freshness one might find in a brand new tube of toothpaste just taken from its box, with its promise of a crisp morning.

His eyes firmly on the girl's rear, Hanio entered the shop without a moment's hesitation. The young woman stopped in front of some sweaters that were part of the clearance sale. The variously colored garments lay in a jumbled heap inside what looked like a sandbox.

Hanio observed the girl's profile as she threw herself into choosing a sweater. She was pursing her lips. The tawdry silver pineapple earrings that she wore even though it was still daytime suggested she made her living in a third-rate bar. However, from the side her features were attractive and he found the curve of her nose exquisite. Women with drooping noses made Hanio sick of life, but this nose was shaped in a way that revived the spirits.

"Would you like to go to a café?" Hanio asked artlessly, almost as if it was too much effort.

"Wait a moment. I'm looking at this right now," the young woman answered coolly, without so much as a look at him.

She reached deep into the pile and pulled out a sweater. Spreading the arms of the garment wide so that it took on the appearance of a large black bat, she appraised it. Her pursed lips suggested she was not particularly impressed. A label with a garish red and gold company logo dangled from the sweater's torso like a fancy strip of paper you might see at the summer Star Festival.

"It's not a bad price . . ." she said out loud. She then turned to Hanio for the first time. "What do you think? Does it suit me?" She held it up to her chest for him to see.

Hanio was surprised by her easy tone: it was as if she were conversing with a man she had been living with for ten years. At the same time, he noticed how the sweater, which had resembled a lifeless bat, swelled out when placed across her chest and clung there wantonly.

"Not bad," said Hanio.

"OK, I'll buy it. I won't be a minute." The young woman went to the cashier. If she had asked him to buy such a cheap garment for her, it would have made him feel like a husband buying some gift to placate his wife. Hanio enjoyed watching her from behind as she peered into her purse and made her purchase.

They found a nearby coffee shop and went inside.

"The name is Machiko. I assume you want to sleep with me?" she said.

"I'm still deciding."

"Oh, you're awful! How spiteful you are!" she said with a great gust of laughter.

Everything went just as he'd hoped it would. Machiko did not have to go in to work until seven in the evening, so he went with her to her sparsely furnished apartment a few blocks away.

Machiko yawned, and undid the hooks on the side of her skirt. "I never feel the cold," she said.

"Well, you weren't wearing a coat, so I knew you had to be hot."

"Oh yeah? You're a cocky one, aren't you? I know your sort," she said.

Her body smelled so strongly of dry grass from the countryside that Hanio worried afterward that he might have some of it stuck in his suit.

19

After sharing a light meal in a snack bar, he saw her off to work. They went their separate ways and he sat through half a yakuza gangster film. When he got back to his apartment, it was just after eight.

As he stepped up to open the door, he almost tripped over something. Someone was crouched down there in the dark.

"Hey, who are you?"

A diminutive, thin boy in a school uniform stood up without replying. His small, dark face resembled a rodent's. "Are you really sold?"

The question was the last thing Hanio expected, and for a moment he couldn't take it in. "Eh?" he asked back.

"Has your life really been sold?" There was an increasing stridency to his tone.

"It's as it says on the card."

"Not true. You're clearly alive and well, aren't you? If you actually were sold, you'd have to be dead."

"Not necessarily. Anyway, come in."

For some reason, Hanio had already taken a shine to the boy. He ushered him inside. He then switched on the light and lit the stove. Meanwhile, the boy looked around, making sniffling sounds like young people do. Without sitting down he said: "Very strange. You don't look like you've got money problems, so how come you want to sell your life?"

"Don't ask things that don't concern you. After all, everybody has their own reasons." Hanio offered him a chair.

The boy made a big show of flopping himself down. "Ah, I'm exhausted. I was waiting for two whole hours."

"I'm already sold, so what else would you expect?"

"I saw what you had written on the other side of the card. I'm sure you just turn it over when you want to take a break. Even I can tell that much."

"That's very sharp of you. So, does a kid like you have the money to buy my life?"

"This should do it." The boy undid the gold buttons of his school jacket, casually pulled out a bundle of ten-thousand-yen bills from his inside pocket as if he were producing a travel pass, and held them under Hanio's nose. It had to be about two hundred thousand yen.

"How did you get hold of that?"

"Don't worry, I didn't steal it. I sold one of the Tsuguharu Fujita sketches in my family's possession. I got a pittance for it, but I had no choice. It was an emergency."

The way this pitiful youth with his rodent-like features spoke made it abundantly clear he was from a well-heeled, respectable family.

"Now that's a surprise. I stand corrected. So what do you intend to do with my life once you've bought it?"

"I'm a son with a powerful sense of filial duty."

"Very admirable."

"My dad died some years ago, and my mother raised me, her only child, all on her own. On top of that, Mother has had her own poor health to contend with. It's all been so sad."

"You mean, for your mother?"

"That's right."

"So, what do you want of me?"

"To put it in a nutshell, I want you to look after my mother."

"You want me to nurse her?"

"She's ill, but she'll recover right away with care from you."

"But why is it necessary for me to sell my life?"

"Let me explain, will you?" The boy stuck out a beautiful red tongue and licked his lower lip. "The sad fact is, when Dad died, Mother became sexually frustrated. At first she held herself back out of consideration for me, but it wasn't long before she just couldn't resist anymore."

"It happens," Hanio interjected. He felt slightly bored.

This callow little schoolkid clearly had some excessively grand illusions of what life was all about. He was at that age where they construct strange and tawdry dramas in their heads, convinced they know all there is to know. But there was something about the boy that was rather precocious. You see it a lot in young people these days. Something dry and tasteless, like the stalk of an overgrown blade of grass—that's how it seemed to Hanio. He's come to buy my life out of a desperate need to act like a grown-up, Hanio thought. He found it hard to take him seriously.

"Then, Mother got herself a boyfriend. But the guy didn't stay around for long. She found another one and he escaped too. There must've been twelve or thirteen of them altogether. After being with her, they all turned white as a sheet and hightailed out of there. And then two or three months ago she was dumped by a man she was head over heels about, and she found herself unable even to get out of bed. She went down with chronic anemia. Can you guess why?"

"Mmm," Hanio replied, not particularly concerned. The boy's eyes sparkled as he came to the point.

"Can't you tell? My mother is a very unusual sort of person. You see, she's a vampire."

20

What did the boy mean? How could his mother be a vampire? Did such things as vampires really exist in this day and age?

But the boy offered no further explanation. Instead, he punctiliously produced a printed receipt with clear instructions. "I've entered two hundred and thirty thousand yen here, with an additional note: 'Strictly advance payment only. Reimbursement due in case of buyer dissatisfaction.' Sign here, please." He handed over the receipt.

"I'm a bit tired today," the boy announced after taking back the receipt, now signed. "I need to go to bed. I'll come for you tomorrow at 8 p.m. I suggest you have an early dinner. Make sure all your personal arrangements are in order before leaving. After all, you might not return alive. And even if you do make it home in one piece, you'll be away for about ten days, so be prepared."

Alone, Hanio recalled the name at the top of the receipt he'd been asked to sign. Kaoru Inoue. Somehow death seemed more likely this time round. Hanio thought it best to get a good night's sleep himself.

The next evening, at eight o'clock precisely, there was a knock at the door. It was Kaoru come to fetch him. Like the day before, he was wearing his school uniform. The boy seemed surprised at Hanio's cheerfulness. As they left the apartment, Kaoru tried to ascertain whether Hanio knew what he was letting himself in for: "Do you really hold your life so cheaply?"

"Yes."

"What did you do with the money I gave you yesterday?"

"I put it in the drawer."

"You didn't deposit it in the bank?"

"What would be the point of that? If somebody finds it after I'm dead, all that will happen is my landlord will pocket it. Surely you get what I mean? You can value my life at two hundred or three hundred thousand yen: it's all the same to me. Money only makes the world go round when you're alive."

The two left the apartment and started walking.

"Let's get a cab." The boy seemed in a buoyant mood as he hailed a taxi.

Once the driver had received instructions to go to Ogikubo, it was Hanio's turn to ask a question: "You seem in remarkably good spirits. Does it make you happy that I'm about to die?"

The driver's startled eyes flashed up in the rearview mirror.

"Of course not. I'm just thrilled to be able to do something positive for Mother."

It dawned on Hanio that the boy viewed everything through the lens of his fantastical world. But his two previous adventures had both ended in tragedy, so he was relaxed about taking part in an absurd comedy this time.

The taxi stopped outside a magnificently gated house tucked away in a dark residential street. Since this was where the boy got out, Hanio assumed it was the place, but Kaoru kept on walking. After turning left and walking for two or three more blocks, he used his key to unlock the door of a house much like the earlier one. He looked up at Hanio through the darkness and smiled sweetly.

No lights seemed to be on in the house, but the boy continued to unlock yet more doors until Hanio found himself in a well-lit reception room.

The musty room that met Hanio's eyes in the light of the floor lamps was an elegant one, arranged in a traditional style and with a real fireplace. A cracked Louis XIV mirror hung above the mantelpiece, below it a gold-colored antique clock with supporting cherubs on either side. Kaoru gave a sneeze, and silently set about getting the fire going.

"Are you and your mother the only ones living here?"

"Of course."

"What do you do for meals?"

"These domestic questions are really boring. I see to the cooking myself. And I ensure my patient gets properly fed as well."

With the fire flaring up beautifully, the boy picked out a bottle of fine brandy from a corner cabinet. Holding two brandy glasses by their narrow stems, he skillfully warmed them in the flames of the hearth and then held out one to Hanio.

"What about your mother?"

"Oh, she'll be another thirty minutes or so. We have this arrangement. Whenever anyone enters the front door, a bell rings by her bedside. After that, it takes her a while to get out of bed and put on her makeup and clothes. So it'll be thirty minutes minimum before she appears. Mother has taken rather a shine to you, and she's a bit on edge. You take an excellent photo."

"My photo? How did you get hold of one?" Hanio asked in surprise.

"Didn't you notice? I took one yesterday evening."

The boy showed him a small camera, roughly the size of a matchbox, poking out from his jacket pocket. He smiled teasingly.

"Well, I didn't see that one coming." Hanio rolled the brandy about in his glass, and then sipped it. Its fragrance encouraged him to imagine that tonight's encounter might contain something sweet. Kaoru gazed at this adult doing what adults always do—enjoying a relaxed drink after his meal—and fiddled with the buttons on his jacket. Suddenly he sprang to his feet.

"Ah, I forgot. I have some homework to do tonight. So I will leave you now. Please be nice to Mother. By the way, I know an undertaker who's not at all expensive, so you need have no worries in that regard."

"Hey, wait a minute!" Hanio said. But the boy had disappeared.

Alone, Hanio could only kill time by looking around the room. Why was he always in this situation, waiting for something to happen? This must be what "living" was all about. While he was working at Tokyo Ad, it had actually been more a kind of death: a daily grind in an over-lit, ridiculously modern office where everyone wore the latest suits and never got their hands dirty with proper work. Most likely, those colleagues would think it oddly contradictory now to discover Hanio, who had determined to die, sipping brandy and looking forward to the future, even though his own death featured prominently in it.

He cast his eyes idly around the room. A pen and ink fox-hunting drawing. A portrait of a sallow-looking woman . . . His gaze alighted on a packet peeking out from the corner of a picture frame. People often tuck secret stashes of money in such spots, but surely, he thought, no one would hide money in a reception room. It was a long wait, and Hanio's curiosity gradually got the better of him. Finally giving in to it, he went up to the picture and removed the packet.

Its coating of dust was proof of how long it had been lodged there. Perhaps someone had knocked it out by mistake when dusting the frame. Surely it couldn't have been deliberately placed there to catch his attention?

The packet contained several pages of manuscript paper, the type students use to write their essays. As he looked through them, the dust smudged his fingers like the dark residue that comes off a moth's wings. There were some lines of writing:

"Poem to a Vampire" by K

Hair disheveled
Absolute self-contradiction disheveled
Rusty abandoned car by the riverside in springtime
Such erotic ecstasy and
blood
You grind your teeth instinctively on the gorgeous
  liquid
Night is enclosed
in each and every capsule
When swallowed as a tablet
a lyrical cockerel breaks into song
At the entrance to the Excelsior Hotel
(the hotel's throat)
a policeman with serious inflammation of the heart
drags out a red carpet
Delicious, absolute, revolutionary rules
To these rules the Vampire Party holds fast

These lines of unintelligible nonsense had been written out in quite awful handwriting. It was a poem one might describe as surrealistic, perhaps: but the propensity for obscurity it revealed was outmoded. Who on earth could have written it? The handwriting suggested a man, but surely no man of any sophistication. Hanio yawned and went on to read the poem that followed simply to pass the time.

All of a sudden the door opened. A thin, beautiful woman entered the room.

Hanio was astounded by what he saw.

She looked about thirty and had a willowy body. Despite her beauty, however, she was clearly not at all well. She wore a brilliantly green kimono, with an obi belt of the deepest blue.

"What's that you are reading? Ah, that . . . I wonder, who do you think wrote the poems?"

"I wouldn't know . . ." Hanio replied. He didn't really want to say.

"It's the boy. Kaoru."

"Oh, young Kaoru."

"I think you'll agree, he's not particularly talented. I was reluctant to throw them away; that's why I kept them. But I have no interest in poetry and the like, so at some point I tucked them behind that picture there. How did you find them?"

"I saw them poking out from the edge of the frame . . ." Hanio hastily stuffed the bundle of papers back where he'd found it.

"I am Kaoru's mother. It seems that Kaoru has recently benefited from your kindness. I am most sorry for all the inconvenience we have caused you."

"It was no inconvenience."

"Please come nearer. Why not sit here, by the fire? I'll get you another brandy."

Hanio did as she had suggested, settling into a lightly padded chair. His elbows rested comfortably on the armrests. The decorative brass studs in the fabric of the chair glittered in the light of the flames.

He felt like a schoolteacher who had come for a chat at the home of the PTA Chair.

The woman sat herself opposite him, her own glass of brandy in hand. "Thank you for coming. I hope you can help." She raised her glass as she spoke.

On her finger a large diamond sparkled, engorged with reflected red light. Her facial features stood out clearly next to the fire, and the flickering flames lent them an air of agitation, only enhancing her beauty.

"Excuse me for being so direct. But did Kaoru tell you something strange?"

"Yes. No. Well, what I mean is—"

"How terrible! He's a smart boy, but he's such a dreamer. And in my opinion, they don't teach them anything useful these days."

"You may be right there."

"What *do* they teach them at school? That's not to say that education in the past was absolutely perfect. But I would prefer schools to provide more instruction about social responsibilities, and manners, so that they knew the proper way to treat others. As things stand now, we pay out the school fees, but all the teachers seem to be doing is preparing their students to become political agitators and union members."

"I couldn't agree with you more."

"And of course, these days everywhere gets bone-dry with all the central heating. Tokyo is not especially cold, but you'd think we were living in the far north."

"Yes, that's the way it is in those modern high-rise blocks. I much prefer this kind of traditional fireplace."

"You say the nicest things." She laughed, her eyes smiling. Even the tiny creases around those eyes were beautiful, he thought.

"Here at home, we try to rely on natural sources of heating as much as possible. And in summer, we avoid air-conditioning. I've heard that the method they use to heat high-rise buildings these days dries out the air so much that before you know it you're bleeding from the throat. What a terrifying thought!"

Ah, we're finally getting to the point. Hanio's heart skipped a beat, but she returned straightaway to more mundane matters.

"People always harp on about how unhealthy life is in the city. And to a certain extent they are right to do so. Civilization has gone too far, and we're suffering from terrible car pollution. On the other hand, the garbagemen just never come."

"Garbagemen these days are lazy good-for-nothings."

"Exactly. I must say, you strike me as very sympathetic to all the problems a housewife has to deal with. Men these days are a funny lot. You know, it's quite surprising, but it's only the bachelors who seem to be aware of all the difficulties involved in looking after a house. The married men end up quite oblivious to everything. You are single, aren't you? I'm sure you are."

"Yes."

"From your youth, I imagine that you must be at the peak of your physical powers. May I call you Hanio?"

"Please do."

"Thank you, Hanio. Incidentally, what about all the fuss that's going on these days about Kusano Tsuyuko—that divorce that's in all the papers? The weekly magazines are just buzzing with it."

"Well, she's a movie actress—what do you expect?" Hanio meant, with the tone of this response, to indicate his lack of interest in such gossip. But she seemed not to catch on.

"Oh yes, well . . . I always thought she had a dream marriage—why does she suddenly want a divorce? The weeklies put it down to the husband's infidelity, of course, but surely that's not all there is to it. You have to remember, that woman was born and bred in Kyoto, which of course means she keeps a tight grip on every penny her husband earns. I imagine she must have been very strict with his pocket money, and he obviously grew tired of being under her thumb. A wife should be as kind and generous to her husband as possible, in my opinion—give him as much free rein as possible. What do you think, Hanio: are you aware of what's really going on?"

"I have no idea," Hanio replied brusquely.

He was becoming bored and losing patience. Until that moment their chairs, separated by the fire, seemed quite a distance apart. It was only when her hand suddenly touched his on the armrest, as if swooping in from above, that he realized they were sitting just a few inches away from each other. Her hand had been right by the fire, but it was icy cold.

"My apologies. My chatter bores you, I'm sure . . . Do you watch movies much?"

"I do, but I only like yakuza ones."

"I see. Of course, cars are the latest thing for young people, aren't they? It's all the magazines seem to go on about these days . . . But reckless driving terrifies me. I can't imagine anything more senseless than dying in a car accident."

"Indeed."

"All I hope is that the Governor of Tokyo will fix the traffic congestion in the city once and for all. I once encountered a person who had been seriously injured in a car accident on Highway One, the one linking Tokyo and Yokohama. The ambulance didn't come for ages, and everyone got in such a state. And all the while, blood was pouring out of the body. All they had to do was get him to a hospital quick and give him a blood transfusion. But then again, you have to be careful about purchased blood. It can give you hepatitis."

"That's true."

"Have you ever donated blood?" Her eyes caught the reflection of flames from the fire.

21

"No, I can't say I have."

"Well, don't you think you might be neglecting your duty to society? Think of all the people in the world suffering from a shortage of blood. As a fully grown man, don't you feel you ought to be ready to lay down your life for someone who may be in need?"

"Actually, all I want is to lay down my life! That's the very reason I came here tonight!" Hanio's feelings were so pent-up that the words burst out of him.

"Of course. Of course." She gazed at Hanio's face, smiling faintly. He shuddered involuntarily in response.

After a brief silence, the woman spoke again. "I assume, in that case, that you will be staying the night."

It was late and the house was entirely quiet. Kaoru was doubtless already fast asleep.

She led him up to the first floor, to a Japanese-style bedroom at the rear of the house. It was not the sickroom he expected. The pervasive smell was of cold and mildew rather than of the woman who regularly slept there.

"I'll just light the heaters."

One by one, she lit the portable heaters set up in three locations in the bedroom. The room immediately filled with the strong smell of kerosene fumes. The thought of these unstable heaters all falling over at once, like three collapsing towers of fire, passed through Hanio's mind.

A high bed consisting of three thick futon mattresses, one on top of each other, had been laid out on the floor. The woman was a little unsteady on her feet when, after undressing to her underwear, she got into bed. Hanio gave her a hand.

"I've been so anemic recently that I often get dizzy fits." She spoke as if to cover her embarrassment.

A high-quality but threadbare silk coverlet had been thrown on top of the bed. The mattresses seemed to have received very little airing at all, which bothered Hanio. They should have been light, but their padding had become so dank that they felt unbelievably dense.

As Hanio gently removed her underwear, he was amazed at how youthful she looked. Was she really that boy's mother? She had the look of a woman of barely thirty—but perhaps that was down to her skill with makeup. Her skin was white and smooth, tight and cold like porcelain. He could see no sign of wrinkles or a fading complexion, but the skin lacked the taut fullness of life. It had the pleasant fragrance of a candle, and yet it seemed completely unconnected to life itself. Something emanates from within the human form and lights up the whole body, but that vital element was missing in her. There was a lustrous quality, for sure, but it was the lustre of a corpse. The faint boniness of her arms betrayed her extreme thinness. And yet her breasts were full and firm, while her stomach was soft and white like a vessel brimming with an abundance of rich milk.

Hanio had become extremely aroused and went to embrace her. But after submitting to his caresses for a while, almost in a daze she twisted and turned her body like a serpent and squirmed out of his arms. Before he knew it, Hanio found himself underneath.

He ended up in that position without any sense of having been humiliated, however. She had very skillfully slipped out from under him and now lay on top, a move she had accomplished without the slightest injury to his male pride, as deftly as a snake might wriggle out on top of a strawberry leaf.

Hanio felt oddly dazed. He caught a faint whiff of alcohol, and realized he was being given a swab. Was that a scalpel in her other hand? He intuitively closed his eyes and felt the icy scorch of alcohol on the skin of his upper arm. A pain shot through him.

"Arms first. My, what strong arms you have." She spoke in a whisper. The next instant, a different kind of pain arose as she closed her lips around the wound and sucked on it. There was a long moment of calm. He distinctly caught the gentle sound of the woman swallowing something. It was his blood, Hanio realized, and a chill ran through him.

"That was delicious. Thank you. That's enough for tonight."

The woman's lips, smeared with blood, came toward him under the light from the floor lamp, in search of a kiss. Her cheeks were now glowing vividly as they had been earlier when she sat close to the flames. The color of abundant life. Her eyes overflowed with the same normal, healthy vitality you might see in any young woman walking down the street . . .

22

Hanio decided to settle into the house for the long term.

Night after night, she sucked the blood out of him. One after another, various parts of his body came under her knife, as she cut open his veins. The more she drank of it, the more she seemed to crave.

One afternoon, he caught sight of her poring over a chart of the human body, with her back to him. The chart had detailed drawings of all the veins and arteries in a human body marked out in red and blue. The sight sent a chill running through Hanio, even though he had known from the start what he was letting himself in for by coming to this house. For her, he was no more than a body for her research, no different from one of those diagrams.

But for the most part, he found life in the Inoue household to be extremely pleasant.

In the morning when the sparrows began to chirp and dawn light started to show in the windows, Hanio would sense as he lay there drowsily that the woman was leaving the bed. He would slip back into sleep. She was going down to prepare breakfast for her son.

There had been a complete turnaround in her health since he moved in. It was hard to credit she was the same person. An early riser, she would get up and almost immediately start humming to herself. Having seen her son off to school, she would return to bed, and at the sound of her footsteps Hanio would finally awaken. With each morning, her face appeared ever more radiant and healthy.

Kaoru too was in much better spirits. Alone with Hanio, he would chat away.

"What an absolute bargain you were! You're the best thing I ever bought in my life. I don't even regret losing the Tsuguharu Fujita sketch, even if it was a memento of my dad. Mother has taken almost no time to recover—she began to improve from the first night you stayed over. She makes me proper breakfast in the mornings, and the whole house feels more cheerful. She and I are getting on a lot better too. I'm even feeling much happier in myself. It's all thanks to you, Hanio.

"But there's still something that bothers me. Now that we've finally found someone so perfect for Mother and me, what'll happen when you die? I couldn't bear it if you did die, Hanio, and I'm convinced Mother feels the same thing deep down . . . She's falling for you, which means she'll inevitably end up killing you before long.

"Until then, I beg you, don't desert Mother. Please let's go on living in this amazing way, the three of us together. I've always dreamt of being part of a happy family like this."

Hanio was surprised at how pleased and proud Kaoru's words made him feel. Whenever they all ate dinner or sat cozily together in front of the television, Hanio would find himself succumbing to the illusion that this was, indeed, an ideal family.

Kaoru was a very diligent student. Even while watching TV he would have his English study book open on the table, and during commercials he would be leafing through its pages. As for his mother, she was hardly recognizable, she had so much energy. She threw herself wholeheartedly into her household duties, preparing delicious dinners in the evening, making sure to include liver, meat, and eggs for Hanio, to keep up his strength. She cleaned and polished the old house from top to bottom, and in the evenings she would do her knitting, her beautiful supple fingers clicking away with the needles as she watched TV. The smiles that graced her cheeks suggested she was divinely happy. Hanio took up his old habit of poring over the newspapers, whose words had once seemed like lines of cockroaches to him.

On occasion, they would go out together. But this was always as a couple, never individually.

When they left the house, the woman bound Hanio's right wrist to her left wrist with a delicate gold chain, which she would only remove when they got back to the house. The chain was so small that it escaped public attention, but she only needed to give it a slight tug for it to dig into his wrist and convey some message she was trying to send him.

Hanio began to find it too much effort to leave the house. The thing was, he truly enjoyed lounging around at home, basking in the family atmosphere. On the other hand, his body was becoming distinctly more sluggish with every day that passed. He was losing the will to get himself out.

Whenever he felt lightheaded after making a sudden dash to cross a road, he realized that his time was running out. He didn't feel alarm at this exactly: it was more as if everything was becoming too much of a bother.

And yet—it was so strange—he didn't feel any fear, nor for that matter any hankering for life. He grew progressively sleepier and more listless as the days grew warmer, and there was every sign that his condition would become even more pronounced as he entered the new season.

One day, they made a visit to Hanio's old apartment. He thought he ought to pay the rent.

The super came out of his office. "Where on earth have you

been? Do you have any idea of how worried I was? Why disappear like that? . . . But you look absolutely terrible. Are you sick?"

"No."

"What a shock you gave me. When you came in just now, you had the face of a corpse."

The super, who liked the ladies, was distracted by the woman, who was snuggling up to Hanio. He clearly wanted to take Hanio aside and ask him what the deal was, but the gold chain prevented Hanio from giving a frank answer.

"I just need to get into my apartment for a moment."

"Be my guest. After all, the apartment's still yours."

"I thought I would pay for the second half of the year in advance."

Once the couple had entered the apartment, Hanio took a look in the small drawer he had left locked. The two hundred and thirty thousand yen were still there. There was still such a thing as decency in this world, it seemed.

The woman offered several times to pay his rent, but Hanio refused. He handed over one hundred and twenty thousand yen to the concierge and got a receipt.

He and the woman conversed in low tones.

"You're too conscientious," she said.

"No, I'm just handing things out to people to remember me by. After all, I have no relatives."

Hanio checked that the "Sold" card was still up. Then he went back home with her, carrying a large stack of mail that had accumulated in his absence.

He was glad to find himself with some reading material. But when he started to look through the mail, his eyes began to smart and flashes of white swirled across the pages. In recent days, Hanio had been shocked by his pale and sickly appearance when he caught sight of his reflection in the mirror: when shaving, for example. But he realized his anemia had got so bad that he could not even make out words on the page.

"What's wrong?"

"I have a little problem. My eyes are blurry and I have difficulty reading."

"You poor thing!" Her voice, however, was quite cheerful. "Shall I read them for you?"

"No, thank you."

Needless to say, they were all quite inconsequential letters. One was from an old classmate. And there were several letters from people he did not know at all, such as this one:

> I don't know who you are, sir, but I saw your "Life for Sale" ad and thought it must be a joke. I simply had to let you know what I thought of the matter, and that is why I am writing this letter.
>
> Are you not aware of the old saying "Our body is a gift from our parents. In gratitude, we keep that body safe"? I suppose you are not. Anyone who places such an ad in the newspaper must be quite without education.
>
> What on earth do you hope to attain by holding your life so cheaply? For an all too brief time before the war, we considered our lives worthy of sacrifice to the nation as honorable Japanese subjects. They called us common people "the nation's treasure." I take it you are in the business of converting your life into filthy lucre only because, in the world we inhabit, money reigns supreme.
>
> Personally, I resent this world where money drives everything, but it is precisely because of human trash like you that financiers can lord it over us. Let me be blunt. Your ad is abhorrent. It represents the very worst of moral turpitude . . .

The letter continued in this vein for at least another eight pages. Hanio could just imagine some pushy, ruddy-faced middle-aged man, out of a job and with lots of time on his hands. With some effort, Hanio managed to tear up the letter and toss it aside. His fingers had very little strength left in them.

Another letter: this one from a woman, and littered with misspellings:

> You're quite cool, aren't you? Really cool. You come straight out and say laif for sail [life for sale?], so I guess that means you have the rest of your laif wurked [worked?] out. I'm selling my laif too, so why don't we trayed [trade?] and go beddy-byes as if we're already intimate? Next morning, we can discover laif together. We'll grab the joy of human laif. Let me blow your whistle while we run among the blossoming rose buds. Would you like to marry me?

A few of the other letters contained similar requests.

Once he'd read them all, Hanio was so exhausted that he had to ask the woman to tear them up for him. Unlike his own fingers, hers were graceful and strong and they flushed at the tips as she ripped the thick bundle of letters effortlessly into tiny pieces.

In bed that evening, unusually serious, she put her mouth to his ear. "I'll have Kaoru stay over at a relative's house tomorrow."

"Why?"

"Because I want the two of us to be free to enjoy ourselves to our hearts' content."

"But don't we do that every night anyway?"

"Tomorrow evening will be special."

She laughed. He caught the scent of blood as her warm breath brushed his nose. "Tomorrow evening, I really want to make sure Kaoru is not involved in any way."

"But will he be willing to stay somewhere else?"

"Oh yes. The boy's not a fool."

"So, what's the plan?"

She paused for a moment. Her hair, which had grown even more lustrous lately, gave the illusion of swelling in the dim lamplight. "This may sound terrible, but I'm a little bored with the blood from your veins. It tastes insipid, and doesn't hit the spot for me anymore. Tomorrow evening, I've decided, it'll finally be time to move on to your arteries."

"So this is it, then?"

"Yes . . . I've been wondering for a while which of your arteries to go for. The carotid arteries give the best result, I believe. I've always thought you had a lovely thick neck. I wanted to sink my teeth in as soon as I laid eyes on you. But so far, I've always managed to restrain myself."

"Please, it's all yours."

"Thank you. How happy you make me feel! You're so sweet. You know, I believe you are the first real man I've ever met. That's why I've decided . . ."

"Decided what?"

"After feasting on your blood tomorrow night, I'm going to knock over the kerosene heaters and set the house on fire."

"And what will happen to you?"

"Silly. I'll just go up in flames."

Hanio closed his eyes. He had never before experienced anything like this in his life: a true meeting of hearts.

His eyelids twitched. He was not used to this . . . Before he knew it, it was the next evening.

23

"Shall we go out for a walk, our very last on this earth together?" said the woman.

That day, they were both going to meet their deaths. For winter, it was a beautifully warm evening. Kaoru had already been sent off to a relative's straight from school.

"There's a small park in the neighborhood," she continued. "It takes its name from the Musashi Plain, and the elm trees look beautiful with their bare boughs. I would love to look at them one final time."

"Couldn't I just stay at home?"

"But I want us to take a walk and share one final memory together. Like a couple of young lovers."

"All right, but no longer than thirty minutes, please."

The truth was, Hanio now found it really irksome to go out for any sort of walk. He just about had the physical strength to stand provided he had a pillar or something to lean on, but even then he was so weak he became lightheaded. A stroll in the park was the last thing he wanted. He felt unbearably sluggish, and having his arteries cut open was preferable to continuing in this state of semi-wakefulness.

"And I'd rather people didn't see how pale and wasted I am."

"Nonsense. You really have the ideal, perfect look. I don't know why, but men can never understand how attractive that is. It's so romantic. Truly. It's just how I imagine Chopin to have been."

"Enough of that. I don't have TB."

While they joked and chatted, she changed into her leather walking gear and then approached him, gold chain in hand. Hanio had chosen to wear a loud apricot-colored sweater which he hoped would give his complexion a little more color. He left the house with the slender gold chain around his wrist, like a dog being led out for its walk.

Once outside, he felt much better. Invigorated by the air, he inhaled every breath so deeply that it made his body sway. The thought that this was the last time he would ever view an evening landscape made it all the more precious.

"Was there ever a time when I really loved life?" he wondered.

The fact that he even had to ask such a question indicated his total lack of self-confidence. Right now, he could feel a love of life growing within himself, but that might be put down to his lightheadedness and poor physical condition.

The beauty of the evening sky pierced him. He felt his heart thumping erratically, and his temples throbbed. Soon, a cluster of giant elm trees loomed into view, their wintry branches, like beautiful lace, stretching over the roofs of this residential district.

"You see that? Those are the elms I was referring to earlier," the woman said. "The park is famous for them."

So he was finally to die tonight. Hanio was looking forward to it. What particularly pleased him was that it was not going to happen by his own hand. Suicide was actually harder than people think—too dramatic for his taste. And if you were going to get yourself killed, it would have to be for some reason. No one had ever detested him or resented him that much, and anyway, the thought that he might be of sufficient interest to others that they would want him dead horrified him. Selling your life was such a splendid way out: it took away all need for responsibility.

The tops of those beautiful elms captured the pale shades of the evening sky in such an exquisite way. A net spread across the heavens: that's what it looked like. But what did it all mean? Why was nature so beautiful for no reason at all? And why did people worry themselves about such trifling matters?

But that was all in the past now. The thought that his own life was about to cease cleansed his heart, the way peppermint cleanses the mouth.

They passed a tobacconist's kiosk at the park entrance. In front of it was a red mailbox. An old lady sat tending the kiosk.

That was as much as Hanio remembered.

The next moment, a white tornado whirled up the back of his head. He grew dizzy and almost collapsed. He thought he could feel someone trying to hold him up with their hands, but then everything went blank.

24

When he came to, he was in a hospital bed. It was already night, and a plump nurse was reading a magazine spread open under a shaded lamp.

"What the hell happened to me?" Hanio asked. Despite an intense ringing in his ears, he could make out the nurse's words.

"Ah, so you've come round. Please relax. There is nothing to worry about."

"What on earth happened? I know I collapsed by the tobacconist's . . ."

"It was a serious case of insufficient blood flow to the brain. You fainted. The woman at the tobacconist's must have called an ambulance—it was an ambulance that brought you here. They said it was an emergency."

"Another ambulance?" Hanio's heart sank. And then: "Well?"

"Well what?"

"What was the diagnosis?"

"Serious lack of red blood cells. The doctor was amazed. When he took a blood sample, yours was quite yellow and seemed to consist mostly of water. He was surprised you could even go for a walk in the state you were in. Based on all the indications, he concluded you must be one of those people who make a living donating blood, but you'd taken things way too far this time. Yet you didn't look the type. And then, of course, you were accompanied by your beautiful wife."

"Oh, where did that woman go?"

"What are you saying? You mean she wasn't your wife?"

"Where is she?"

"She went home. I'm sure she felt you were in good hands once she heard from the doctor what was wrong with you. You'll get back to normal provided you stay in the hospital for about a month, fortify your blood with the right medication, and take nutrients. She said she had something to do at home. That was about three hours ago."

"Have I been unconscious all this time?"

"No, that would have been a cause for real concern. The doctor mixed a sedative in with your serum and nutrient injections. After all, the most important thing is rest. Complete rest. No activity or excitement."

"But . . . She . . ."

"I must say, she seemed a very caring woman. And so gorgeous and healthy-looking too. It was just like she'd sucked all the energy out of you!"

Hanio was lost for words.

"Before she left she made an advance payment for one month's stay in the hospital, by banker's check. She was most kind—she even gave me a generous tip . . . That's how I know you're not a professional blood donor."

Hanio remained silent, his eyes shut. Then, a sudden thought hit him, and he leapt up with a cry.

"What's the matter? Please, no sudden movements."

"I've just thought of something dreadful. It's an emergency. Call her. Now. Please."

Hanio gave the nurse the Inoue family telephone number. After insisting once more that he lie down, she dialed the telephone at his bedside. Hanio waited uneasily. His heart began to pound again.

"There's no one there."

"Is it ringing?"

"Yes."

The moment the nurse put down the receiver, he heard the wail of a fire engine siren start up in the distance.

"Oh dear. There must be a fire somewhere. There hasn't been a drop of rain round here for ages, so it doesn't take much for a fire to break out."

Hanio listened in silence as the siren came closer. Another siren started up somewhere else and the two sounds became entwined.

Hanio could not contain himself. "Where are we now?"

"Eh?"

"What's the location of this hospital?"

"Ogikubo. The hospital was built on the highest part of town, and is well known for the splendid vistas it offers of the area. Even long-term patients don't complain, because they get such great views. It's more like a hotel, if you ask me. And this room is one of the best."

"Can you see the district where she lives from here?"

"I think so. It should be just beyond the park."

"Yes, of course. Please, stick your head out of the window and tell me if that's where the fire is."

The two wailing sirens grew louder. After insisting one more time that he should not overexcite himself, the nurse went to the window. She opened it slightly and took a look.

"Oh! I can see it," she cried. "The fire is definitely coming from that district."

Beyond the crook of her arm, Hanio saw a sky so red it made her white uniform grow crimson. Wildly, he tried to get out of the bed, but dizziness overwhelmed him and he lost consciousness.

25

Despite repeated inquiries, he found it impossible to learn about the fire in any more detail.

A plainclothes police officer, a detective by the look of him, visited and subjected him to a brief interrogation in the doctor's presence. Hanio was going to have to come clean about his relationship.

"So what was your relation to the deceased?" the detective asked, his foul-smelling breath reaching as far as the bed.

"I was a friend."

"While out walking with her, you fainted and were brought here. Correct?"

"That's right, but you've got to tell me, what on earth has this—"

Before the doctor could signal him to stop, the detective began to fill Hanio in with the dry facts of the situation.

"Mrs. Inoue was burned to death in a fire that started in her house last night. She had a reputation for loose morals, and whenever there is a fire with a single fatality, questions are always raised. Her only son is with relatives at the moment, but it was pitiful the way he clung to his mother's corpse and wept. Apparently, his school grades are really outstanding . . . Anyway, you have a perfect alibi and you're under no suspicion yourself. I'd simply like you to answer a few questions."

Hanio was surprised to find himself, who had never lamented anyone's death, weeping as he listened. Where did these tears come from?

"All I can say is, I loved her." Hanio spoke with feeling.

"We're not questioning what she might have left you in her will, or anything like that."

"Please. Don't be so vulgar."

The doctor whispered something to the detective.

"Right. Well, look after yourself." With these parting words, the detective left to go back to the police station.

The elderly doctor addressed Hanio in a soft voice, looking down at him in his bed. "It's all got rather complicated. But the most important thing for you is to stay absolutely calm and recuperate. Your hospital fees have been paid in advance, with some to spare. And I believe the lady's final wish was for you to rest so you could return to your former good health as soon as possible. You're young, and you'll get through it all without this unfortunate incident doing lasting damage. Even medication depends on your frame of mind. Sometimes it works, and sometimes it doesn't, right? What better way to remember her than by starting out on a new life in a positive frame of mind. Right, now it's time I gave you your sedative."

Hanio felt well disposed toward this man who reminded him, as much as anything, of a wizened old stag. He seemed more like a pastor than a doctor. Hanio recalled similar commonsensical words of encouragement being given him on a previous occasion.

The details were different, but someone had used almost identical phrases when he left Accident and Emergency after he had taken his overdose. Those words had encouraged him to throw himself headlong into daily activity and live life to the full. Of course, whether or not he was willing to take such advice was a different matter!

26

Despite his worries, Hanio was young enough for his recovery to be relatively speedy. It became clear that he wasn't going to have to stay a whole month in hospital after all. He could probably leave in two weeks, the doctor told him.

One day, Kaoru dropped in. Hanio felt rather reluctant to look him in the eye, so afraid was he of the kind of recriminations he might receive. But Kaoru seemed quite happy. He spoke very freely, despite the nurse's presence.

"Hanio, I came because I wanted you to know how grateful I feel for what you did. I know all sorts of investigations are being carried out into Mother's death. Did she kill herself? Was it arson? Did the fire start accidentally? But whatever the outcome, Mother is dead. There is nothing we can do about it.

"When I think about it now, I believe she just couldn't stomach life. And I've come to the opinion that we should simply treasure those happy memories when the three of us were living together. At least with you alive, Hanio, we can share those memories from time to time. And above all, thanks to you, I believe that Mother went to her death having tasted true happiness for the first time. I have so much to thank you for."

While the young man delivered these words, which would normally be expected to come from the mouth of an adult, large tears fell from his eyes onto the knees of his school trousers.

"Come and visit whenever you want," said Hanio. "Feel free to speak to me about anything."

"Oh, thank you."

"Ah, there's a small favor I'd like to ask of you. Fortunately, I still have the key to my apartment in my possession. I had it on a key ring which I kept in my trouser pocket, so it wasn't destroyed in the fire. Sorry to trouble you, but if I gave you the key would you be willing to go and check my apartment?"

"Oh. So you're going to start all that again?" The boy took a step back. "Please don't! How could you? Haven't you learned your lesson yet?"

"Don't worry. Just go and take a look. I imagine there's a whole stack of mail behind the door. All you have to do is pick it up for me."

The boy agreed and took his leave. Immediately, the nurse started pumping Hanio for information.

"So what kind of work do you do?"

"I don't think that's any of your business."

"I'm just curious to know."

"I'm a male escort. But I guess you could tell."

"Really? I expect you're far too expensive for me."

"I offer a free service to young ladies."

"Goodness . . . !"

The nurse rolled up the hem of her white skirt to reveal white garters around the tops of her white stockings, and above that, her fleshy thighs, which were tinged with the tan coloring of countryside clay.

"Wow! Is that what they meant when they said you get a good view in this hospital?"

"Maybe. So, are you getting your strength back?"

By way of reply, Hanio took the nurse by her arms and pulled her onto the bed . . .

It was some time before Kaoru came back. Hanio had been getting worried, but just after dinner the boy turned up.

"That was terrifying," he said, throwing the mail onto the bed.

"What was? The nurse has already gone home today, and no one else is coming, so you can relax. Tell me what happened."

The boy was out of breath. "I opened the door and was rummaging around when two guys burst in."

"Japanese guys?"

"Yes. But what's that got to do with it?"

"I just had a feeling they might be foreigners. And then?"

"One of them grabbed me from behind and asked if I was the one who put the ad in the newspaper. I almost stopped breathing. The other said I was just a kid, so it couldn't be me. Then the first man complained how they'd been coming day after day, and just when they finally thought they'd caught their guy, they end up with a child. At that point, the other man suggested that I was probably running an errand for you, and it might be a good idea to force me to reveal your whereabouts. He had a scary voice. I pretended I'd tell them everything they wanted, but instead I grabbed the mail and fled back here . . ."

The boy suddenly stopped speaking, and his mouth opened wide in terror. The door of the room had slowly swung open without warning.

27

Two men rushed in.

"Who are you?" Hanio spoke calmly.

To describe him as "calm" implies something of the heroic. But in fact he was perfectly at ease with the possibility that these men might dispense with him at the drop of a hat. In his heart he still harbored a wistful desire to follow in the traces of that beautiful vampire: a desire that threw into question his earlier frivolous yet pragmatic attitude toward death. But what did any of this matter? Who cares about the motives of someone about to die?

One of the men stood just inside the door, with his back to it, keeping guard over the room, while the other kept his eyes fixed on Hanio as he lay in the bed.

Young Kaoru cowered against the wall on the other side of

the bed, so that Hanio appeared to be shielding the boy with his own body.

The men appeared to be both in their thirties, one slightly older than the other. Their actions were not quite flamboyant enough to mark them out as yakuza. The steeliness in their expressions and their rugged features suggested they probably started off in the military or as police officers. Well, they're certainly nimble on their feet, Hanio thought, but their dress sense leaves something to be desired. He was even tempted to advise one of them that a tired mouse-gray tie never works with an ash-gray suit.

"Right, let's get started." The elder of the two men, who seemed to be in charge, did not take his eyes off Hanio as he spoke to his companion. This second man, who had been by the door, approached the bed. As he did so, Hanio noticed that the first man was holding a black gun in his hands, and the muzzle was pointed straight at him.

"Don't move. And keep your trap shut. Got it? . . . And if the kid squeaks or tries to escape, he'll get a taste of this."

Rather predictable script, Hanio thought. But then, to his surprise, the man who had approached him now perched himself on the edge of the bed. He grabbed Hanio's left arm by the wrist, and began carefully to measure his pulse.

Thirty seconds of silence passed.

"Well?" said the first man.

"Thirty-eight in thirty seconds," replied his companion. "That makes a rate of seventy-six."

"That's not very high. It's completely normal, isn't it?"

"A normal pulse is a little bit lower. With some people, it's even around fifty."

"Right, then." The first man pushed the cold muzzle of the gun up against Hanio's pajamas, just where his heart was. "Listen to me. In three minutes, I'm going to pull the trigger. If you move or make a noise before then, I'll shoot straightaway. Otherwise, you'll at least have three minutes to live."

Kaoru began to whimper.

"Stop that!" the man growled under his breath.

Kaoru fell into a heap on the floor weeping soundlessly.

The first man indicated with a glance that his companion should take Hanio's pulse again. Silence, like a black river flowing by.

"What is it now?"

"That's odd. It's gone down. Sixty-eight."

"Impossible. Take it again."

"OK."

Hanio felt as if he was undergoing a medical checkup for his heart, and he gradually started to relax and enjoy it. There was something inexpressibly funny here. He simply could not be bothered to put up a fight.

"Well?"

"Still sixty-eight."

"OK. He's got nerves of steel, this one. I'm amazed. First time I've seen anything like it. It was worth all that effort to hunt him down."

The man tucked his gun away in his suit, and then spoke to Hanio in an entirely different, gentle tone.

"Please make yourself comfortable. It was just a little test, which you passed with flying colors. That really was amazing. That's quite some nerve you have. Stupendous results."

The man stepped back to pull up a chair and sat down by the bed, looking quite friendly now. With the unexpected change in circumstances, Kaoru stopped crying and emerged from the shadow of the bed.

"Would you mind telling me who you guys are?" said Hanio.

He noticed the third button of his pajama top was undone. As he did it up, he felt something jab his fingers. He took it out and examined it. A gleaming hair pin. The nurse must have dropped it there earlier.

"Ah-ha. Quite the ladies' man." The first man grinned and lit a cigarette.

"I asked who you were," Hanio repeated.

"We hope to be clients of yours. We want to buy what you're selling."

"What?!"

"That's not a very nice way to address your clients. After all, we've come to purchase the very thing you've put up for sale. Is it so strange that potential clients should turn up on your doorstep?"

28

"Couldn't you have thought up a less troublesome way to hire me?"

Hanio was exasperated. He fumbled to light a cigarette. The first man took out his pistol and pulled the trigger. Out popped a flame, which he held right under Hanio's nose.

"So it was all a silly game."

"Well, there are all sorts of tricks you use when testing someone," the man replied with a kindly expression that suggested he was, at heart, a good person.

"I hope you'll forgive us, kid," he said to Kaoru. "Sorry about having to rough you up a bit earlier in the apartment. We felt we had to pull out all the stops—we simply had to get hold of Hanio here as quickly as possible. It's not as if we had any other options, and we knew Hanio couldn't give a fig about his own life."

"What does 'give a fig' mean?" Kaoru asked timorously.

"Give a fig means give a fig. You mean you've never heard

that expression before? Honestly—schoolkids these days! No wonder people slag off education in Japan now . . . Come on, boy, time to go home. Hanio is quite safe—we have no intention of doing anything illegal. And don't snitch to the police on the way home. If you try anything, I might well have to exchange this toy pistol for a real one. I bet you wouldn't enjoy going to school with your stomach full of daylight!"

"If you pumped my stomach full of holes, I'd fit the holes with lenses so people could take a peep for ten yen a time. It'd be a good way of getting pocket money."

"Stop your funny stuff and get yourself home."

"Goodbye," Kaoru murmured, looking anxiously at Hanio.

"I'll be fine. Don't worry. You were pretty pushy too, eh, when you first visited me at my place? I'll be in touch again soon, so rest easy and go home."

"OK." Kaoru's shadow disappeared round the door.

"So you mean that kid was a client too?"

"It was actually his mother who bought my life."

"Wow!" The first man seemed incredibly impressed. His companion sat himself down on another chair, finally assured, it seemed, that it was safe to relax.

"Now, if you're going to talk to me about something you didn't want the boy to hear, shall we have a drink to go with it?" said Hanio. "I've actually been advised by my doctor that alcohol is good for me. Some patient, eh?"

Hanio produced a bottle of Scotch from under his bed, with some glasses. He roughly wiped the dust off them with his sheet, and handed one to each of the men. They listened apprehensively to the glugging of whisky as he poured it into the glasses.

The three raised their glasses and drank solemnly.

"Right then, to business," said the first man. "A reward of two million yen if you're successful. In the event of failure, you just keep the advance payment of two hundred thousand. How does that sound?"

"You mention a reward if I succeed, but succeeding will mean I forfeit my life. So what you pay me will amount only to two hundred thousand."

"Don't jump to conclusions. If this job goes well, you won't have to pay for it with your life. You'll get the two million."

"So give me the lowdown." Hanio sat cross-legged on the bed and sipped on his drink as he settled down to hear their story.

29

"Where to begin?"

As the first man started to speak, Hanio noticed the creases around his eyes, testament to both hardship and a heart of gold.

"Neither our names nor our occupations can be divulged. You will understand, of course, given the nature of what we are asking you to do. In any case, as you see, we are Japanese. But in fact our story has nothing to do with Japan. Rather, it concerns the embassies of two other, quite different countries. Let's call them Country A and Country B.

"Now, the wife of the ambassador of Country A is a renowned beauty, and one evening she held a party at the embassy to which she and her husband had invited ambassadors from various nations around the world.

"For an embassy, such an event is no more extraordinary than if you and I were to invite guests round to play mahjong. That evening, the ambassador's wife greeted the guests wearing an elaborate emerald green evening dress with a long train. An imperial prince was in attendance, so it was a black-tie party with everyone in full regalia. I am not at liberty to disclose the nature of our connection to this particular event at the embassy.

"Now, as you will appreciate, an evening dress embroidered in emerald green requires accessories in exactly the same color. The wife of the ambassador of Country A was in possession of an exquisite necklace—a most wonderful piece that comprised thirty-five magnificent emeralds interspersed with small diamonds. The dancing began, the lights in the banqueting hall were dimmed, and the guests were swept up in the flow of things. But as the party drew to a close, the ambassador's wife suddenly noticed that the necklace was no longer draped around her neck. She kept her composure, and hardly any of the guests realized what had happened. Those who did notice merely assumed she had removed it at some point.

"Half the guests had left early while the dancing was still in progress, so the ballroom was already quieting down as the party came to a formal end. Slightly pale, she nevertheless saw each person off with a brave smile. When the last guest had left, she fell sobbing into her husband's arms.

" 'Oh, this is terrible! Just terrible! My emerald necklace has been stolen.'

"The necklace had cost an absolute fortune, so this was a serious theft. But, she explained, she could hardly have created an embarrassing scene over its sudden loss right there in the middle of the party when she was entertaining all those guests.

"The ambassador himself turned white at this news, stunned. This man was by no means a stingy person. Indeed it was said that he had a considerable fortune back home, and had only taken up the role of ambassador as a hobby. There was no reason he should get upset over just a necklace. But the truth was, the ambassador had a serious problem that he had kept even from his wife.

"To clarify what I mean by this, let me explain a little about the emerald as a precious stone. Most jewels are valued in accordance with the flawlessness of their surface. It is only with emeralds that this is not the case. An emerald is always naturally flawed—it has what they call 'inclusions.'

"These inclusions are one of the emerald's natural charms: the effect is often likened to peering into an utterly green sea. There is even aesthetic value that accrues in the different configurations produced by the flaws. You might say that emeralds, unlike diamonds, have something sensual about them. If you consider these dark internal fissures as giving this beautiful green gem its life force, it isn't hard to go one step further and imagine that the emerald embodies some sort of organic mystery.

"Now, when the ambassador first made a gift of this necklace to his wife, one man-made emerald had in fact been placed in among the natural ones. The artificial emerald was truly splendid, so perfectly formed in terms of its fissures and coloration that it was impossible to distinguish it from the other thirty-four.

"However, in reality, the flaws in this single man-made stone had been deliberately structured in such a way as to form a cipher key that allowed the ambassador to decode the highly classified telegrams that his home nation, Country A, would send him personally to read. This particular emerald constituted a prism. Light passed through the maze of smoky dark fissures, and was refracted onto the surface of the telegram so as to rearrange the writing into intelligible lines.

"The ambassador had earlier become aware of someone intercepting the telegrams sent to him from his home nation, which was why he came up with the idea of inserting this cipher key into the one emerald. He arranged with his wife to keep the necklace in his care and whenever she required it for a party or some such event, he would take it out of the safe. She, of course, was unaware of the secret.

"Noticing how pale he had turned, she said. 'Who could it possibly be? Imagine—taking such a thing so brazenly from under my nose. And to think that tonight's guests were limited exclusively to ambassadors and to Japan's most distinguished ladies and gentlemen.'

" 'When do you think it was taken?' A slight quaver was discernible in the ambassador's voice.

" 'During the dance. No other time would have been possible.'

" 'Whom did you dance with? How many people?'

" 'Five, maybe six.'

" 'Try to remember. All of them.'

" 'Well, the first was the prince.'

" 'I think we can leave him out. Who else?'

" 'Next was the foreign minister of Japan.'

" 'It wouldn't have been him, surely. Next?'

" 'The ambassador of Country B.'

" 'Now, it could have been *him*.' The ambassador bit his lip.

"A ruthless espionage battle was being waged in Tokyo between Country A and Country B, so naturally the ambassador of Country B seemed the obvious suspect. People had been tipsy, the room was crowded and only dimly lit, and the music had been in full swing. The ambassador of Country B might be a big fatso but he had absurdly delicate fingers: he was quite capable of loosening the necklace from around the slender white throat of the wife of the ambassador of Country A without her being aware of it.

"That night, the ambassador and his wife tried to decide whether they should inform the police, but they could not make up their minds. As day broke and they found themselves exhausted from lack of sleep, a servant came in with a silver tray, on which lay a plain brown envelope.

" 'This came through the letterbox this morning, sir.'

"They opened it to discover the emerald necklace inside. Needless to say, the ambassador's wife was deliriously happy.

"'Someone was obviously playing a prank on us. But how very cruel of them! Whoever it was, they ought to feel thoroughly ashamed of themselves. What diplomat would carry out such a ruse?'

"'Are you sure it's the same necklace?'

"'Yes, quite sure.'

"She held out the beautiful thirty-five-emerald necklace so that it caught the light of the morning sun and jiggled it slightly. The ambassador took the necklace from her and looked for the emerald that concerned him. He could tell immediately. That stone had been exchanged for a natural emerald."

30

"Things might have worked out a little better if the ambassador had revealed the secret of the emerald to his wife there and then," the first man continued with his story. "But in this regard the ambassador was a true gentleman of the old school. No matter how energetically his wife helped him with his official embassy business, he preferred to keep highly classified information entirely to himself.

"The ambassador immediately sent a telegram to his country requesting that, since the cipher key had been stolen, all future coded telegrams should be reformulated in an entirely new way. With that he had resolved any problems that might arise in the future. But there was still the problem of telegrams that had been sent already. If they were intercepted, decoded, and their contents made public, this could well trigger a major international incident. There was no doubt in his mind that some other party had become aware of the emerald's secret and had stolen it.

"If the material was decoded and revealed immediately, the

ambassador reasoned, the situation would already be irredeemable. But a delay of one day would mean a ray of hope—and nothing happening in two days or more would ensure that the ray became even stronger. Such a delay would suggest that the other party feared retaliation in the event of publication, or at the very least that they were aware of some other reason why it could not be revealed.

"But even if that were the case, he would never be able to get them to return whatever material they had stolen. And anyway, whoever had taken it would no doubt immediately have made lots of copies to send back to their own country. Even if he managed to get one set of copies back, it really wasn't going to solve anything.

"The ambassador was pulling his hair out. Every day he felt on tenterhooks. There seemed no other option but to await their next move. But no! He suddenly realized he had one trick left up his sleeve.

"If Country A were to steal Country B's cipher key—that is, Country B's equivalent of Country A's emerald—it might be possible to do a deal. Country A was already busily intercepting telegrams being sent from Country B, but for the moment they couldn't make head nor tail of the code.

"There wasn't a day to lose. The ambassador decided he should take the initiative and steal their key as quickly as possible. The only question was: where was it?

"Country B had managed not only to identify Country A's most closely guarded secret—their emerald key—but also to swipe it from under their very noses. This had of course only been possible thanks to the magnificent, renowned spy network of Country B. But Country A had its own espionage system that the ambassador knew to be every bit as good. It was surely only because they had not put their minds to it that they had not yet found the secret key being used by Country

B. The ambassador put out word to his spies that Country B's key must be tracked down and seized within two days.

"Country A's spies had been keeping the embassy of Country B under surveillance for quite some time already, but they had found nothing in particular that set it apart from other embassies. There was only one possible distinguishing feature: the ambassador of Country B had the habit of staying up late at night in his library to study. Maybe it was then, the spies wondered, that the ambassador of Country B decoded the telegrams sent from his own country. The ambassador was also famous for being inordinately fond of carrots. On his desk was a glass filled with about twenty carrot sticks, which he would sprinkle with salt and munch on whenever he was hungry. Country A's spies had obtained this information from a vegetable shop that provided the Country B embassy with a constant supply of the very best carrots.

"Breaking a secret code—and carrots. Now, that combination almost makes you laugh!

"A certain spy of Country A, someone exceptionally skilled at what he did, found himself wondering if this combination might be not entirely fortuitous. Let us call this man—the first to infiltrate the Country B embassy—Agent X1. Though born in one of the smaller nations of Europe, he had received a thorough education in espionage in Country A. He belonged to no one nation, however, and was in possession of eight fictional personal histories.

"Before he found his way into the embassy of Country B, Agent X1 met secretly with the ambassador of Country A.

" 'I am confident I will find the key tonight and deliver it to you,' he told the ambassador.

" 'What's your plan?'

" 'I will sample the carrots of the ambassador of Country B,' the man said, brimming with self-assurance.

"This was the last time the ambassador ever saw Agent X1 alive. He was discovered dead in the embassy of Country B. It was announced in the media that a thief of unknown origin had broken into the embassy and had committed suicide there, with potassium cyanide. There were no further developments in the matter.

"Several days went by, and the ambassador of Country A was somewhat relieved to see that the embassy of Country B still had not released the contents of the intercepted confidential telegrams. But of course this did not give him complete peace of mind. Country B might be aiming to make things public in a month or even a year, waiting for the most politically opportune moment.

"The ambassador of Country A called in a second man, Agent X2, to poke around. He too disappeared under similar circumstances. Word had it that, just like Agent X1, he also met the ambassador of Country A before taking his leave and informed him: 'The carrots hold the key.'

"And then another man, Agent X3, disappeared in a similar fashion. Finally, the ambassador of Country A had no option but to acknowledge how serious matters had become. Obviously there was something going on with the carrots. It was said that the ambassador of Country B had the supply replenished every night, but no one knew exactly why. Moreover, from the scant information at his disposal, the ambassador of Country A surmised that the agents had all got as far as stealing a carrot stick from the bunch in the glass on the desk, but the moment they put it in their mouths, they died on the spot—with symptoms, apparently, of potassium cyanide poisoning. This would suggest that maybe only one or two of the twenty carrot sticks in the glass were without the poisonous coating. But only the ambassador could tell which ones they were, allowing him to pop them in his mouth and crunch away to his heart's content. Even though it was pretty clear that the carrots were the clue to the cipher key, there was no way of telling which of the twenty sticks were free from poison.

"I might also add that the three spies who had died were what they call intangible cultural assets, each of whom cost millions to train. The ambassador of Country A could hardly sacrifice any more such experts to no purpose.

"So, this is where you come in. We want you to smuggle yourself into the embassy, identify which carrot stick is not poisoned, take a bite, and by doing so obtain the key to break the code. How does that strike you?

"As you see, we are Japanese, but we feel grateful for what Country A has done for us, and that's why we wish to buy your life and so repay our debt."

"If things go well, I suppose you'll end up with a huge reward, too," said Hanio.

"Naturally. If that weren't the case, we wouldn't have come chasing after you pretending to be gangsters when we're old enough to know better."

"I see." Hanio nonchalantly blew a puff of cigarette smoke toward the ceiling.

"Well, how about it? You have a one-in-twenty chance. Do you think you might pull it off?"

"Actually, there's something else going on here . . ." Hanio said, clearly lost in thought. "You said just now that the Country A embassy has been intercepting copies of Country B's top secret telegrams for some time, right?"

"Yes, of course."

"If I can hazard a guess, they are completely worthless in that form."

"Why do you say that? As long as we find the key . . ."

"No, we should direct our attention to the paper, not the key. Has the embassy of Country A managed to obtain any of the paper on which the embassy of Country B receives its telegrams?"

"I'm not sure."

"You need to make sure. We'll have to wait till tomorrow to find out, I guess. I might be dying then, so let me at least get a good night's sleep. All right: go home now. Come and pick me up in the morning."

"What if you were to run away from us? No, tonight we're staying put."

"As you wish. The nurse might get a turn when she comes to take my temperature in the morning, but I suppose I can pretend you're relatives who came to visit and stayed overnight. Rather unwelcome relatives . . . So we're agreed. Tomorrow morning one of you needs to go to the embassy of Country A first thing, and check if they have any paper from Country B in their possession. Until then, there's nothing to be done."

Hanio spoke confidently, then yawned broadly. He settled down on the pillow, and before long he was snoring.

"He has nerves of steel," said one of the men.

The two overnight guests exchanged glances, full of admiration.

31

Next morning, it was a perfect spring day, and quite cloudless. Hanio managed to wangle a permit from the doctor to leave the hospital. While the first man was away at the embassy, he used the time to quietly shave his beard before the bathroom mirror.

With his companion away, the second man suddenly sprang to life and became talkative. His admiration for Hanio was all too clear, but everything he said was unbelievably banal and clichéd.

"Hah, such readiness in the face of death is commendable. You have the heart and soul of a warrior."

For breakfast the man enjoyed a cream bun, which he had got the nurse to go out and buy for him. Hanio watched in fascination as he crammed it into his guileless mouth and as he bit into the bun a crescent of yellow cream oozed out from the side like the rising sun.

For the first time in ages, Hanio had encountered something about human life that tickled him. From what he could deduce, some spies from Country A, one of the most advanced nations in the world, had been responsible for some momentary but catastrophic oversight, and this had led inexorably to their own deaths. Of course, whether he was correct in his deduction remained to be seen.

When he applied shaving lotion, his reflection in the mirror looked so youthful and radiant that even he found it captivating. He had the face of a self-indulgent young man from a family of means, without a single care or responsibility in the world. Outside the window, partially opened cherry blossoms swayed in the breeze.

The first man came back, out of breath.

"Great news. They do have some of the paper in question. The spies of Country A are assiduous in their work. Ah, that reminds me. You've been asked to meet the ambassador of Country A before you go on your do-or-die mission and break into the embassy."

"What time should I go and meet him?"

"They said any time between ten and eleven."

"Right." Hanio looked at his watch. "I have to drop by somewhere first, so I should be able to get there at ten thirty."

"What do you mean, you have to go somewhere? Incidentally, you have some soap behind your ears."

"Thanks." All this uncalled-for interference had distracted

Hanio this morning. But now he rubbed behind his ears with a towel and, while he was about it, wiped his chin. Some drops of red were left on the towel. He had nicked himself with the razor.

The blood brought back memories of the vampire woman, and his heart tightened. Probably never again would he be able to savor that sense of deep immersion in a languid, sweet bath of death. Quite possibly, it was in order to bestow that very favor upon him that she had purchased his life.

"Where do you have to go?" The first man pressed him for an answer.

"No questions. Just come with me. I've some shopping to do, that's all. A certain amount of preparation is required if you're going to kick the bucket."

At a loss how to respond, the man adopted a serious expression. This amused Hanio.

As he left the hospital, his nurse warned: "Now don't go on the rampage just because you're going out. You're not being formally discharged yet."

"I think I managed to prove to you yesterday that I'm a hundred percent healthy."

At this, the nurse pinched Hanio's arm. Even the tingling that this left had more of a sparkle outside in the spring sunlight. The three of them might have been a group of friends off to the horse races as they walked down the broad slope toward town, a mixture of amusement and tension in their faces.

"We need to go to a quality greengrocer, one with only the freshest vegetables," announced Hanio to his two companions. "Somewhere around Aoyama, perhaps."

They hailed a taxi and all climbed in.

It was a while since Hanio had been into town. Signs of death were nowhere to be seen. People were soused in everyday life right up to their necks. You might say they walked around like human pickles.

"When I'm in that world, I'm a sour pickle," Hanio thought. But even as a pickle, he had never amounted to more than an appetizer served with a drink. The dull routine of three solid meals a day was not his bag. "That's fate for you. What can you do?"

At K— store, Hanio bought some carrots that had already been peeled and cut into sticks, and he had someone place them in a polyethylene bag that was frosted from being kept in the fridge. The two men looked on with serious expressions.

"Is that all you're buying?" said the first man.

"Yup," Hanio replied. "Right then, let's go to the embassy of Country A."

Hanio's pride was a tiny bit hurt that they had to enter through the tradesman's entrance at the back of the splendid chalky limestone embassy. Passing through the kitchen, they ascended a grubby stairway. They opened a door and immediately came into a magnificent Edwardian-style study.

His two companions stood to attention.

On the opposite side of an imposing desk sat a distinguished-looking gray-haired gentleman. He was sitting very straight.

"Sir, we have brought the person we mentioned."

"You have done well. I am the ambassador of Country A." The gentleman courteously extended his hand to Hanio. When Hanio shook it, he felt as if he were grasping a dried flower. It seemed so soft that the merest grasp would crush it. Even so, he imagined numerous thorns sticking into his own palm.

"Here is the advance," the ambassador then said.

A check lay on the table. The ambassador quickly filled in the amount to be paid, two hundred thousand yen, signed his name, and gave it to Hanio before the ink had even dried.

"Right, Ambassador, let's get right down to business," said Hanio. "Is that blank paper you have there from Country B?"

"Yes, it is. We got some ready for you."

"Could I please ask you to get someone to type out one of the intercepted telegrams from Country B, making sure it fits neatly within the borders of the blank sheet?"

"Of course."

The ambassador rang a bell to summon the typist, and handed her a copy of one of the intercepted telegrams and the blank sheet of paper.

"I've got a copy of the telegram here," he said to Hanio. "Have a read."

Hanio could tell at a glance that the telegram consisted of a meaningless jumble of words. Even if it were translated directly into Japanese, it would make no sense.

As they waited for the typist to do her job, Hanio, the ambassador, and Hanio's two companions sat facing each other in complete silence. The wall was decorated with portraits of major politicians from Country A, and the desk was surrounded by bookshelves with gorgeous old leather-bound editions, among them *The Collected Works of Benjamin Disraeli*. A sickly-sweet odor redolent of Westerners hung in the air.

The rather formal, middle-aged typist showed no expression as she returned with the typed sheet, before taking her leave.

"So . . ." said the ambassador.

"Right." Hanio took one of the carrot sticks from the still icy polyethylene bag and tossed it into his mouth.

32

The color of carrots comes from carotenoids, which can be converted by the body into vitamin A. The deeper the carotenoid pigmentation, the more abundant the potential amount of vitamin A. The one constituent in carrots that works to destructive effect is the enzyme ascorbinase, which breaks down vitamin C. On the other hand, carrots contain no starch whatsoever. Consequently, the saliva-based enzyme ptyalin, which changes starch into maltose, has no effect on carrots.

Hanio had a hunch that the secret to ungarbling the letters might be found in the ingenious way in which ascorbinase and ptyalin, two elements that have no effect on each other, combined. There had to be some connection with the reciprocal reactions of these two elements with other chemicals that coated the telegram paper. Where ascorbinase has no effect, ptyalin would produce one chemical reaction, and where ptyalin has no effect, ascorbinase would produce its own separate chemical reaction.

Hanio gave the carrot a good chew, then spat the masticated mush out onto the telegram and smeared it about. They watched as a coded text emerged from among the words.

"Astonishing!" The ambassador was in code-breaking heaven. He began to nod, and emitted a series of contented grunts. "We have lots more carrots. There are plenty of other telegrams I want deciphered. I'm so relieved. This means we have nothing to fear in our dealings with Country B. They won't know what's hit them. It looks like it's ended in a complete tie."

Hanio was still chewing away. "It could do with a bit more salt. But I think it would work well served as a snack with a drink. Could I trouble you for a glass of whisky?"

"You'll get your drink later, when it's all over. Right now, I wouldn't want anything to affect the chemical reaction." The ambassador's eyes shone with delight as he gazed in anticipation at Hanio, who munched away on the carrots like a hungry horse.

33

Once the chewed remnants of all the carrots had been thickly smeared over all the telegrams, Hanio was led into a separate room where he received a check for a further two million yen. His two companions also received a check each. From the happy look on their faces, it was a hefty sum.

The ambassador offered a whisky to Hanio. "How on earth did you manage to do it?" he asked. "I'm dying to know how you figured out a plan of action that involved no risk to life."

It was beyond Hanio's ability to spell out all the complex details in English, so he asked the elder, more talkative of his two companions to interpret for him. The man was more than happy to step in, and his English turned out to be pretty fluent—far superior to the basic language skills that Hanio had expected. It ought to be said that Hanio did not mince his words, so the man did some editing where appropriate.

"First of all, I'm amazed at how sloppy Country A has been. Losing three key intelligence officers like that—why, that must have cost millions. On the other hand, those guys were complete mugs, so your country's probably better off without them. I'd say your biggest mistakes come down to avarice, obliviousness to the essential simplicity of things, and obsession with trivial details. Am I wrong?

"Three intelligence officers went into the embassy of Country B, one after the other, to try out the carrots. They were on the right track, at least up until that point.

"I should tell you that I had a look at a newspaper article reporting the first death. How did the headline go? 'Dumb Thief Enters Embassy of Country B, Eats Poisoned Carrots, Drops Dead.' The article went on to describe how the victim was found with a piece of carrot laced with potassium cyanide in his mouth. It included the ambassador's explanation that some feed for animal experiments they were conducting had been accidentally left out on the table: the thief must have been hungry and eaten it. Everyone who read the article must have thought it was hilarious.

"Now, this is where you all had the wool pulled over your eyes. And, as a consequence, a second spy suffered the same fate. Your mistake was to believe, even after the first death, that the ambassador of Country B was continuing to place poisoned carrots on his table night after night, and was lying in wait for the next thief.

"But I ask you, did anyone actually see the first spy die after putting a carrot in his mouth? Mightn't someone have crammed it down his throat? The fact is, the ambassador of Country B managed to fool you all into thinking a special carrot was required to break the code you were after. He convinced you that the problem centered around how to distinguish between poisonous and safe carrots. He was running circles round you.

"The moment I heard the story, I could smell a rat. Did it never occur to you that they might be *nothing more than ordinary carrots*? Even a child could have come up with that idea. But you thought it must all be so incredibly complicated that people ended up losing their lives.

"That's why I came here with another plan up my sleeve. First of all, I wanted to conduct an experiment with some completely ordinary carrots. I assumed that most carrots in a bunch would be effective. But if my experiment had failed and I'd ended up having to go and try a carrot laced with potassium cyanide, I would have died without regret. When you're putting your life on the line, there's no use fussing over a few carrots.

"Actually, I might as well admit right now that I loathe carrots. That dull shade of orange—such a crude, boorish color!

And the smell of them—especially when they're raw! Truly disgusting.

"I detested my father, and when I was a child I'd watch him crunch away on raw carrots. I used to think that, if he carried on like that, he'd turn into a horse. And I swore I'd never allow anything so vulgar to pass my lips for the rest of my life. At some point, that childish way of thinking developed into a visceral revulsion.

"As I grew up, whenever I found myself having to eat a beef stew or some such dish that contained carrots, I would be overcome with disgust—it was worse than peering into the depths of a toilet bowl. And if I came across that novel *Poil de carotte—Carrot Head*—by Jules Renard on the shelves of a bookshop, the author's insensitivity would astonish me.

"In short, if I had a choice, I guarantee I'd rather get a hole in the head than eat carrots. But at the present moment, my life lies in my client's hands rather than my own, so I have made an exception and opted, albeit unwillingly, for the carrots. Two million yen is probably about the right price.

"And now a few words for you, Mr. Ambassador. Stop overcomplicating the way you think about things. Life and politics are generally simple, much more simple—shallow, even—than you imagine. Of course, I'm aware that my attitude might be different if I weren't prepared to meet death at any moment. It's only the desire to live as long as possible that makes everything seem complicated and mysterious.

"And now I take my leave. I doubt I'll be seeing you again. I promise never to discuss the work I've done here with any other party, so please refrain from sending any of your fine intelligence officers to keep a watch on me.

"And please do not ask for my help ever again. I'm not going to be any use to you in the future. The petty political squabbles between Country A and Country B do not interest me in the slightest. I imagine it's only because you have too much time on your hands that all you ever do is pick fights with each other . . . Goodbye."

By the time the other man had finished interpreting, Hanio was almost out of the splendid door, his head respectfully lowered.

34

Back at the hospital, he quickly gathered up his belongings and checked out. Taking care that he was not being followed, he went back to his old apartment, and immediately started packing up his things there.

"So you've decided finally to leave? Just when you have made such a good recovery? Well, I'm sorry to see you go. I'm afraid I can't return the half-year's rent in advance you gave me," said the super.

"Keep it," said Hanio.

"For a young guy, you're pretty loaded, aren't you?" The words rolled jealously inside the super's mouth. He seemed to be re-tasting bits of food still caught in there somewhere, like a ruminating cow.

There was not much to pack. Hanio had hardly any books to speak of, and he always threw away clothes that he grew tired of, so all he had to do was to gather together his furniture and pack everything else into three large cardboard boxes. He came upon the toy mouse he had once shared dinner with and tossed it into one of them.

A small removal truck he had booked earlier waited in front of the apartment. The driver gazed idly at a scrawny-looking cherry tree at the entrance to the house opposite. It was the cherry-blossom season, after all. But the tree could not have had more than ten blossoms on it.

Since no help was forthcoming, Hanio brought the furniture down by himself one piece at a time. It may have been that he was not physically back to normal yet, or perhaps the carrots had not agreed with him, but he was drenched in sweat after carrying down just two chairs. The super, lurking somewhere inside, also failed to come to his aid.

As he struggled down the stairs, trying to support the table on one shoulder, he suddenly felt the weight lift off him, and he looked up in surprise to see the elder of his two recent companions lending him a hand.

"Let me help. You're still getting back your strength."

Then Hanio watched as the second of his two former companions came springing nimbly up the stairs. "Do you want me to carry these boxes down?" he asked.

It took no time for everything to be loaded into the truck.

"Thanks very much," said Hanio. "But I told you not to come after me."

"We weren't coming after you," said the first man. "We just thought we ought to help. It's our experience that people always turn tail and try to run away after they've done us some act of kindness. It's perfectly understandable. We'll leave you in peace after this, but if you ever do find yourself in need of a favor, please call us anytime. We'll come straightaway."

"I take it you carry guns?"

"Naturally." The man spoke emphatically, presenting his business card with an expression of genuine integrity. There was a name, Makoto Uchiyama, an address, and a telephone number, but no company position.

"Where are you moving to?" he asked. His expression was the picture of kindly concern.

"No point asking me that. I don't even know myself," Hanio

said over his shoulder as he climbed into the passenger seat. The truck began to move off almost reluctantly, leaving behind the two men waving under the cherry tree.

"Where to?" the driver asked, showing little interest.

"Setagaya." Hanio said the first thing that came into his head.

The truth was, he had no destination in mind. He had two checks in his pocket, one for two million yen and one for two hundred thousand. Gazing out at the spring streets, hazy with pollen, he calculated for the first time how much he had brought in so far since beginning his business: one hundred thousand from the old man at the start; five hundred thousand from the incident that had ended in the woman committing suicide; two hundred and thirty thousand from the vampire woman's son; two million, two hundred thousand from this last escapade.

He had earned a total of three million, thirty thousand yen in no time at all. It worked out to about one million a month. Really not a bad business. His income was ten times what he had earned as a copywriter. He had wasted some money on his apartment, but even what he had left guaranteed him a life of luxury for quite some time.

Of course he would have earned much more as a singer of popular songs or a movie star, but that kind of person had a lot more expenses. No way would their life have been as easygoing as his was. He got lots of attention from people with minimal effort on his part, and he had even had the pleasure of having his blood sucked out of him by a vampire.

It occurred to him that now might be a good time to take a break from this "Life for Sale" business. Why not try leading a carefree and luxurious existence for a while in this part of town? If it turned out that he enjoyed a life that just drifted along with no purpose, he could carry on as he was. And if he decided he would prefer to die after all, he had the option of restarting the business.

There could be no freer state of mind.

He simply could not fathom why people got married and ended up trapped for life, or became company employees working at the beck and call of others. Better to spend all his money. If he found himself penniless, suicide was always there as an option.

Suicide . . .

When his thoughts arrived at this point, he found himself overtaken by a kind of psychological malaise. No matter how you looked at it, he reflected, to kill yourself just because you've suffered some setback required too much effort. If you've finally managed to carve some time out for yourself and flop out, you're hardly in the mood to get up and fetch a cigarette that lies just beyond your reach. Sure, you're dying for a smoke, but it remains just outside your grasp. In fact, it requires a huge effort to heave yourself up and fetch that cigarette: just like when you're asked to push a car that has broken down. That, in a nutshell, is suicide.

"Where in Setagaya?" the driver asked, as they passed along Tokyo's Ring Road No. 7.

"Let's see. Someplace with a real estate agent or employment agency. Anywhere like that will do."

"Are you telling me you haven't decided where you're moving to?"

"Actually, no."

"Unbelievable." The driver did not look particularly surprised, despite his words.

Hanio spotted a real estate agent on the corner of a junction to Umegaoka Station. Stuck to its glass door were slips of paper advertising rooms and houses for rent.

"There. Stop there. Looks like you can park in front."

The driver replied with a muffled grunt.

Hanio slid open the door of the shop with a clatter and was

greeted by the real estate agent, a plump, fair-skinned woman of about fifty. She was leafing through some papers at a desk.

In a corner of the room were a cheap padded sofa and a couple of chairs. There was a vase containing some small artificial roses. A map of the whole district was stuck on the wall.

"I'm looking for a room to rent," said Hanio. "The best would be an annex, or something of that sort—where I could come and go freely without being a nuisance to anyone. Meals included, if possible. Is any such place available?"

"Let's see. Nothing comes to mind immediately," replied the woman. "What's your budget roughly?"

"Fifty thousand a month. Perhaps a little higher. Of course, the cost of meals would be separate."

"One moment, please."

While she was going through her files, the glass door suddenly slid open and a young woman in slacks came in. At the sight of her, the real estate agent openly scowled.

35

The woman in slacks was oddly unsteady on her feet. Though probably not yet thirty, she had a rather coarse complexion. Her features were fine—even chic—but the make-up she was wearing was all wrong for a Japanese woman. There was also a mismatch between her petite body and the breasts that filled out her sweater.

The moment she entered, the older woman seemed to forget that Hanio was there. "Do anything weird, and I'll call the police." The real estate agent fairly bristled as she made her threat.

"Go ahead. I'm not gonna do anything bad." The young woman slurred her speech. She turned one of the chairs round and then fell into it, her back toward Hanio.

"You just stop making such a nuisance of yourself. No one will want your place for the rent you're asking—and with all those ridiculous conditions. I don't care how high the commission is. It's not like it's our job to set you up with people. And even if it were, it would be up to you to find someone and bring him here so we could do the contract. But that would be beyond you, wouldn't it? It's just not going to happen."

"But it *is* your job to find someone for me! You have no right to say such horrible things. You haven't a clue whether I've got it in me or not."

The young woman had barely got these words out before she slumped back in the chair, and was soon snoring away. Her face in sleep was angelic. Her lips were slightly parted and appeared so soft that Hanio was tempted to place his fingers on them. Only her snoring jarred.

"She's acting funny. She must be high on something. Stupid girl! I should just notify the police. Would you mind tending the shop for a minute while I pop out? I'm worried how she might react when she comes round—she might start smashing things up. This is all just too much."

"What on earth is this all about?" Completely forgetting the truck he'd left waiting outside, Hanio sat down. He wanted to hear her story.

"This woman is the daughter of one of the most respectable families in the neighborhood. She lives in a big house with her parents, and she's their youngest. Her siblings are married with their own families. However, as the baby of the family she's used to getting her own way. As a result, she's completely screwed up, and no one in their right mind would want to marry her.

"Her parents started out as wealthy landowners, but at the end of the war they found themselves in straitened circumstances, and they began coming to me to sell off piecemeal the land and buildings they owned. In the end, they were left with nothing more than their own residence. So far, they've managed by hook or by crook to make ends meet through selling off their possessions, but now they're close to rock bottom. The latest idea is to make a living by renting out their tiny teahouse annex, but it's not going well. They just don't accept anything I do to try and help them.

"But it is Reiko here who has really been putting a spanner in the works, and I don't know what to do about it. The deposit she wants for that ramshackle old place is half a million yen, plus a rent of one hundred thousand. She refuses to give way on that. Her other requirement is that the tenant has to be a young, unmarried man. She won't even look at anyone I suggest. I came up with one prospective tenant—a company president, middle-aged, who was willing to pay the asking price because he liked the look of her. But then what did she do when he paid a visit to discuss arrangements but get absolutely wasted! I'm at the end of my rope. Try and put yourself in my shoes. I can't take it anymore."

The idea of going to the police must have slipped her mind. She started to cry with her face buried in her sleeve. In the end, she was sobbing, with her head against the glass door plastered with advertisement slips. The door rattled as she sobbed: probably it was the wind blowing against it.

What with one person snoring and the other weeping, Hanio was flummoxed, but eventually he stood up and placed a hand on the tearful older woman's shoulder. "I think I might be able to help you out."

Wiping away her tears, she stared up at him. "Really?"

"But only if I get something in return. If I'm to help you, I need to be able to stow all my possessions—and I've brought them all with me—in that annex you mentioned. If I don't like it, or if the people in the main house don't like me, I'll be out of there immediately."

"Have you just moved out of another place?"

"See that truck waiting over there? It's got all my things in it."

The wind had picked up, and the truck was parked under a cherry tree that was flailing about on the other side of a fence. The driver had got out and was once more idly taking in the blossoms. A hazy yellow pall tarnished the blue sky. A cat was walking along the top of the fence. It jumped across to the black branches of the tree, scrambled down the trunk, and slunk off, its body pummelled by the wind like a jellyfish tossed by the waves.

It was a strange, bright afternoon. An afternoon in which something gigantic had been misplaced, a spring afternoon that felt empty and full of light.

Hanio had decided to give himself a break, yet here he was again, getting entangled in another bizarre situation. The world seemed so full of multiple twists and turns. No way could the earth be described as a perfectly neat globe, he thought. One moment, the land is pitted with sinkholes, the next moment a plateau suddenly rears up into a perpendicular cliff.

To say that human life had no meaning was the easy part. But Hanio was struck all over again by the huge amount of energy required to live a life filled with so much meaninglessness.

The older woman shook Reiko by the shoulder. "Hey. This gentleman wants to rent your annex. He's young and single, just what you're after. Perfect for your requirements. You should show him round right away."

Reiko's eyes opened, her head resting on the back of the chair, and looked up at him. A single thread of glistening drool spilled from her mouth. Hanio found it repulsive but also strangely erotic.

Reiko struggled to her feet. "At last. Finally, someone worth waiting for." She got up and gave the older woman a hug.

"Can't you try and be happy for me? Why are you always so mean?" Her tone was emotionless and hollow, even if the words themselves were completely over the top.

"This is why I find her such hard going," said the real estate agent, turning to Hanio. "One moment she's a pain in the butt; next thing, she's all sweetness and light." This time, she clearly had her business smile on.

36

Reiko instructed the driver to leave Hanio's belongings by the rear gate of the residence, which was the closest entrance to the annex. She then locked fingertips with Hanio, guiding him along the stepping stones that led to the main house.

They passed through grounds dense with trees; it was hard to believe that just beyond was the heavy traffic of Ring Road No. 7. An elderly couple was sitting together in wicker chairs on the veranda of the main house.

"Ah, welcome home, Reiko," said the old woman.

"Hiya, I've got someone here who's going to rent the annex."

"Well, that is good news! I'm afraid you will find it far from comfortable in our home, young man, but please do come in."

The woman was small and elegant, and she greeted Hanio courteously. The gray-haired old man by her side was obviously refined too, and like her he was dressed in Japanese attire. He introduced himself with a friendly smile that put Hanio at ease. "Pleased to meet you. My name is Kuramoto."

Hanio was led into a formal reception room and seated in the place reserved for a guest of honor, facing the decorative alcove. They served tea. He was treated with an almost inconceivable degree of old-fashioned courtesy.

The furniture was of the highest quality. The thick rosewood shelf in the alcove displayed an incense burner and a cockatoo made of some precious stone. Also hanging there was a picture scroll depicting the legend of the Peach Blossom Spring in the classical style, inscribed with a line of verse.

"Our daughter is not much good for anything, but please don't hold it against her," the old man began.

The old woman picked up the conversation. "And you know, for all her faults, she has the kind-heartedness of a saint. There is something innocent about her. It's only because she's had to struggle in this world, with a heart too pure by half, that she ended up taking Hymena barbiturates."

"Actually, it's Hyminal, Mother."

Reiko took no pleasure in having to spell things out. The mother was describing her almost thirty-year-old daughter as if she were a slip of a girl.

"Ah, is that right? Well, she takes that, and also that drug beginning with L."

"It's LSD, Mother."

"I knew it was L something-or-other. Fine, LSD. Sounds like the name of some sort of instant food, if you ask me. In any case, she takes that drug that's all the rage with youngsters these days, and then she hangs around the Shinjuku area at night. Looking for her Prince Charming. Isn't that right, Reiko?"

"That's enough, Mother!"

But the old woman wouldn't let up. "For some reason the child has a stubborn streak, and that's what differentiates her from her siblings. Her nature is good, and she's always keen to throw herself into everything. I think we should give her all the support we can. What right do old people have to tell young ones what they should do? We've been more than willing to indulge her a bit so she can work out things for herself. Of course I realize it's our daughter I'm talking about, but if someone with such a sweet heart insists on devoting herself to remodeling the annex, and is adamant about having just the right person to live there, who are we to object? And now, she's found you. How lucky for her! It must be all thanks to the gods and the Buddhas. Reiko, why not show him the annex?"

"Sure."

Reiko stood up and once more latched her fingers rather tryingly onto Hanio's, so that he was forced to rise unsteadily to his feet.

The spring sunlight shone abundantly onto the garden through branches with still only a sparse covering of leaves. Skirting the shrubbery where an occasional camellia was in bloom, they made their way back to the annex. Reiko threw open the clattering storm shutters.

He was expecting his nose to be struck by the odor of moldy tatami mats. However, there was no such smell. In fact, unusually for a teahouse, there were no tatami mats to be seen. Instead, the space had been turned into a kitchen with a flooring of clay tiles decorated with an intricate pattern of fallen leaves.

The adjoining reception room took Hanio's breath away. On the floor lay a luxurious Tianjin carpet. A twill bedspread in a Persian design covered a French Indochinese bed fashioned from bamboo, and in the decorative alcove, which would normally contain a scroll and flower arrangement, there was a magnificent stereo system. Nestled in one corner of the room was a set of Vietnamese rosewood Louis XIV chairs decorated with mother-of-pearl, and next to them a stand-alone bronze lamp in the shape of a woman. The lower half of her body was covered in a graceful art nouveau arrangement of lily-of-the-valley leaves, while the upper half twisted to support the light in her hands.

The walls were lined with thick damask, and a beautiful

mirrored wine cabinet was set into a corner. A glance inside the doors revealed an array of exceptionally fine wines.

"Now I see why the rent is so high," Hanio said to himself.

His companion seemed to read his mind. "It's obvious now, isn't it? The real estate agent woman has no idea what the inside of this place looks like. She's a complete idiot. Can you blame me for losing my temper when she goes on at me like that? I've put my heart and soul into creating this place. As you know, I live here all alone . . . Even when I go to Shinjuku, I don't hang out with anyone. And I haven't made any friends. It's only because I'm lonely that I do this. Is that so strange?"

"Not at all. Interesting taste, though. Very unusual."

"All the objects you see set out here come from my dad's collection. I got them out of the family storehouse. Dad was a bit of a bad boy when he was young. But now, he seems to have a more enlightened view of the world."

"Didn't he raise any objections about raiding his collection?"

"Not at all! In this house, my word rules. He's terrified to go against me." And she suddenly let out a shrill laugh that seemed as if it would never end.

There was a knock on the open storm shutter, and the elderly woman entered the room. She held a lacquered tray on which were laid two sheets of ornate high-quality paper, each of them folded in two.

"Here is the invoice and the contract. If you could be so kind," she said.

The documents indicated that the deposit was five hundred thousand yen, and the rent one hundred thousand per month. The words were written in the traditional Oie style of handwriting, which emphasized a flowing script.

"I have the money, but only as a check," Hanio said. "It's past three o'clock now, so would you mind if I went to the bank tomorrow to cash it?"

"Whichever is most convenient for you." And the old woman withdrew.

Hanio suddenly remembered his belongings by the gate. He was worried they might look shabby in a room furnished like this, and wondered whether to have them put into storage.

"If you need any recommendations for where to store your things, I can advise you. I expect you'll need to do something with the furniture you brought with you," said Reiko, unprompted. She seemed to have a knack for reading people's minds.

"How did you know what I was thinking?"

"When I'm high, it just happens. I don't know why. I'm not normally so sensitive."

At that point, they both ran out of things to say, and they fell into silence.

The more he thought about it, the odder this house seemed. It was all so unfathomable. Why had she put together such a gorgeous room, and with such a huge bed? And why was she so fussy about the kind of person she wanted to rent the room to, given how expensive it was?

Of course, she had to make a living, but even so it was hard to believe that a thirty-year-old druggy would just be hanging around a real estate agent's in search of a tenant. She might not be exactly conventional, but she didn't seem to be off her rocker.

It occurred to Hanio that he might be the kind of man who, having just had one close call, was just fated to fall in with another "kindred spirit." People who are lonely have the ability to immediately sniff out the loneliness in others: in that, they're no different from dogs. When Reiko first opened her sleepy eyes at the real estate agent's, she must have immediately registered that Hanio was not your average healthy, practical human being.

The odd thing is that only lonely people have a tendency to festoon their abodes with extravagant items. Hanio was still living in his modest former apartment when he first found success in his "Life for Sale" business, and only after that did he acquire a taste for more luxurious living. Reiko's place suited him down to the ground, not least because its low ceiling lent the room the air of a magnificent tomb.

"I would love to give my mind and body a rest here for a while."

"Why are you so tired?"

"I just am, that's all."

"How can anyone be tired of life, or of the very idea of being alive? It's not normal."

"Well, there's nothing else that makes you tired."

Reiko gave a snort. "I know what your problem is. You're tired of trying to die."

37

Reiko might be having problems focusing her eyes, but her words were weirdly on target.

Hanio was lost for words. Reiko took out a large, sumptuous-looking volume from the bookcase and, resting it on her knee, flipped through its pages.

"Here, look." The book was a large, beautifully illustrated edition of *One Thousand and One Nights*. The picture Reiko was showing him was from a tale about an incestuous relationship. The story concerned two siblings, a brother and sister, born of separate mothers, who were infatuated with each other. They hid themselves from the eyes of the world in a magnificent sealed tomb deep in the ground where they could spend time making love to each other, day and night. Eventually they encountered the wrath of God, and were consumed by heavenly flames.

When the father located their hideaway and entered the tomb, all he found were their charred bodies embracing each other on the bed covered in richly embroidered silk.

A picture showed their naked bodies, now reduced to black coal, but still recognizably human and locked in a sexual embrace, on a splendid, pristine bed without a single scorch mark. It suggested the abomination and ugliness of death, but also the fires of pleasure that had set the couple's beautiful bodies alight while they were alive. The two looked as if they had been consumed not by the fire of heaven's wrath, but by the flames of carnal pleasure that had lit up their lives.

"Burnt to a crisp, but still kissing," Reiko remarked. "What a way to go! They must have died at the peak of happiness."

"Very nice, I'm sure. But what do you hope to attain by installing someone like me in a magnificent place like this?" asked Hanio. "After all, I'm only out for myself."

"I'll tell you, soon enough. I've only ever been looking for one thing, and I think I've almost got it."

38

That night, Hanio had time on his hands, so he telephoned Kaoru.

"Hey, where are you? I noticed you vacated your old apartment." The boy sounded in high spirits. His mother's death seemed not to have left much of a mark on his young heart.

"I moved out in a hurry. So I just thought I'd give you my new address and telephone number."

"You're sure no one's listening in on our conversation?"

"I understand your concern. But who gives a damn?"

"Have you started up your business again?"

"I'm resting at the moment."

"Good, you should take it easy for a while. So is there anything else in your life that's bothering you at the moment?" The young boy was affecting quite a grown-up manner.

"If it all kicks off again, I'll let you know."

"Don't say things like that! Why can't you put your old life completely behind you? By the way, can I come and hang out with you soon?"

"I'm a bit tied up at the moment."

"So you've taken up with another woman?"

"You got it."

"Damn! You're incorrigible!"

"If I get into trouble, I'll give you a call. You're the only person I can trust when things go bad."

These words clearly tickled the boy's self-esteem. "But you'll get annoyed if I save your life, won't you? That puts me in a difficult position. OK, I'll wait for you to contact me. I'll leave you alone for now. Take it easy," he said, and hung up.

The following day, Hanio went to the bank and opened an account. He cashed his check, then returned home and paid Mrs. Kuramoto.

"Oh, how kind! Thank you so much. That'll really make my daughter happy. She's out at the moment . . . She's been looking for someone like you for so many years."

The old woman smiled graciously at Hanio from the door at the entrance to the house. She handed him the contract, which was wrapped inside a fancy purple crêpe covering.

"I wonder if I could consult you on a certain matter?" he asked.

"Of course. Of course. Would you care for some tea?" And she ushered him warmly inside.

Led into their peaceful living room, Hanio instantly felt himself relax. All demons of the modern age had been swept away from that place. All except their daughter Reiko!

Mr. Kuramoto set aside the collection of Tang poetry that he had been reading. "You look well," he said. "Did you manage to get a good night's sleep?"

"Yes, thank you." Hanio nodded gently. There he had been, putting all his effort into hurrying toward death. But here were a husband and wife in no hurry to die. A scattering of cherry-blossom petals, blown on the wind, lay in the garden. In the pleasant midday cool of a shaded room, the old man's white hand turned the pages of his Tang poetry book. These people were taking all the time in the world to weave together their own deaths, calmly, as if quietly knitting sweaters in preparation for the coming winter. Where did such tranquility come from?

"Reiko must be quite a shock to you," said Mr. Kuramoto with a smile. "I am responsible for the child ending up like that. I hope you won't think too harshly of me."

Hanio stared blankly at Mr. Kuramoto. Mrs. Kuramoto brought some tea.

"Go on, dear. Tell him the story," she said quietly.

"A long time ago, I was a merchant seaman," Mr. Kuramoto began. "I rose to the rank of captain, but eventually I left the sea and became an executive in the shipping company, finally becoming company president. I bought up some land around here: my intention was to spend the rest of my life as a major landowner. But we lost the war and it became impossible to make a living as a landlord, and things went from bad to worse. These days, if you really take good care of the land, your assets are worth billions. But things were different right after our defeat: property tax meant I had to sell off a portion of my land, and I continued to sell it off one piece at a time until it was all cashed in. What a fool I was!

"Anyway, Reiko was born in 1939, the year after I gave up being a captain. She was my youngest daughter.

"I had become exhausted by my work as captain. In fact, I'd suffered what these days we would term a nervous breakdown, and I spent three weeks or so in a mental institution. Nevertheless I was appointed a company executive and even went on to have a fine career as president, proof that I had managed to recover from the breakdown with no lasting ill effects.

"However, twenty years later—that would be nine years ago—this mere blip in my own life ended up having very serious repercussions for Reiko. We were in the midst of negotiations for a marriage for her: Reiko was very keen on a particular young man. Suddenly, however, word came from the other party that they no longer wished to pursue it. Now, Reiko is a woman with a fine inquiring mind, and she decided she simply had to find out why she had been turned down, even though there was no real need for her to do so. In the end, it was the woman who'd been involved with the matchmaking who spilled the beans, even though she shouldn't have.

"It seems the young man's side had discovered that I'd been in the hospital for a lengthy stay twenty years earlier. They suspected, quite groundlessly, that the reason must be more than simply a nervous breakdown and, bearing in mind that I'd been the captain of a ship with plenty of temptations around, that I must have been suffering from syphilis. Since Reiko was born the year before I went into the hospital, they surmised she would be certain to have inherited the disease.

"From the moment Reiko found this out, she became a person transformed. She started drinking. She took up smoking. I tried to tell her it was just a stupid story—that the other side was completely deluded but that we could make sure by having a blood test. We could go to the hospital to get a full explanation from the doctor. But she wouldn't listen. There was nothing I could say, no scientific explanation I could offer, that would give her peace of mind. 'In a few years, I'll go insane!

There's no hope for me! I'll never get married, I'll never have children.' That's what she said. And once she started, there was no stopping her.

"Her brothers and sisters all did everything they possibly could to make her see sense. But Reiko became increasingly unhinged and wouldn't listen to anyone. In the end, we transferred the annex over to Reiko and made her the legal owner. That's what she requested. But for some reason, she said that, rather than living there herself, she preferred to rent the room at a high price and live off the income.

"I'm not long for this world, but we have enough funds to support our daughter. As you may be aware, the money received as rent from you will go straight to Reiko and be her income.

"It's a really strange story—I hope you don't mind hearing about it. But in view of the situation, I can only hope you will be good enough to feel some pity for our daughter and decide to stay on.

"Recently, it seems she's been hanging around Shinjuku a lot. She's been taking some weird drugs, and the whole neighborhood has ended up treating her like an outcast. But what worries us more is her conviction she's destined to lose her sanity because of congenital syphilis. We're at our wits' end about how to help. I feel really embarrassed having to tell you all this.

"There is just one crumb of comfort, however. Shinjuku may have become her Saturday night haunt and she might not breeze back home until the morning, but she's always alone when she returns. For some reason, she can't get close to anyone, and as a result she's never brought a single low-life friend to the house. We are eternally grateful for that. It would be so embarrassing to have some disgusting long-haired hippy—someone you couldn't tell was a boy or a girl—popping in and out of our home.

"It's rather forward of me to say this, but you seem a fine, upstanding man, despite your youth. Just how a young man should be."

39

Reiko was taking ages to return home that day. Hanio retired to his bed to read a book, but he couldn't help feeling a bit anxious about how long she would be.

He considered going to Shinjuku to look for her. But that would be pointless. He knew all about these hippy types—he'd had dealings with them during his time as a copywriter. They were seekers after "meaninglessness," all right, but he could not imagine them having the guts to confront the real thing when it inevitably came calling. They'd ended up in their sorry state for quite trivial reasons—a completely groundless phobia about syphilis, for example, or an aversion to school and studying. Reiko was a case in point.

Hanio felt nothing but utter contempt for these people and all the "reasons" they put forward to justify themselves. Meaninglessness never intruded into people's lives the way hippies imagined it would. It always arrived in a form far closer to those lines of newspaper print that had turned into cockroaches.

This was how he saw it. You think you're on a road, walking happily along, but then you realize you're actually balancing on a railing on the roof of a thirty-five-story building.

Or, you're playing with a cat, when suddenly deep in its wide meowing maw, reeking of fish, you see jet-black ruined streets stretching out before you, like the burnt-out remains of a city after a major air raid.

Or, you put a ladle of milk right at the tip of a Siamese cat's nose and, just as it's about to drink, you flip the ladle up to drench its face with the milk. Come to think of it, he'd once been very keen on keeping a Siamese as a pet. But somehow he'd ended up having supper in the company of a toy mouse.

It seemed to him that those very same rituals, so central to his fantasies, were equally influential in every aspect of the Japanese political and economic system. The same impulses drove the way the government's cabinet meetings were conducted: questions of national security were resolved according to the same rituals. It's only when a haughty cat is humiliated out of the blue that we gain insight into the full implications of keeping a cat.

In short, Hanio believed that his ideas were all rooted in meaninglessness and they blossomed into life at the very moment when meaning was created. For that reason, he never once initiated any action on the grounds that it was meaningful. People who ascribed meaning to their actions ended up staring meaninglessness in the face, in a state of frustration and hopelessness. Such people were nothing more than sentimentalists—the sort that couldn't let go of life.

When you opened the cupboard, it seemed to Hanio, meaninglessness was already enshrined there along with the heap of dirty laundry. If you already understood that, what was the point of searching for a life of meaninglessness somewhere else?

Hanio had the feeling he would be offering his life for sale again some time in the future . . .

Just then, the door of the teahouse opened softly. A cat? It was Reiko.

Large plastic earrings dangled from her ears, and she was wearing what looked like a Mexican poncho. Her pale neck protruded from among a blaze of red, green, and yellow stripes.

"Hi." Hanio welcomed her home like family.

"I expect you're starving. Let me make you dinner."

"You provide a pretty good service for a landlady."

"So Father told you, then?" Reiko said, staring at Hanio's forehead.

"That obvious, is it?"

"Yes, I can read your mind." With this comment, Reiko went to the kitchenette and noisily set to work. Hanio was bored and wanted to keep talking, so they conversed together in loud voices above the sound of splashing water and the chopping of her kitchen knife.

"I don't mind coming here to sleep with you from now on," said Reiko.

"That sounds nice, but . . ."

"But what?"

"The thought of us both waking up tomorrow morning as charred corpses gives me the shivers."

"I'll leave the gas on. The explosion will ensure we die a clean death."

"But even in *One Thousand and One Nights*, they only die after satisfying themselves to the full. One night wouldn't be enough."

"Greedy boy."

There the conversation stopped. Hanio heard a saucepan bubbling away in the kitchenette.

"I hope you're not putting poison in that."

"Would that be better?"

"They'll discover the arsenic afterward."

"What'll it matter, as long as we die together?"

"I haven't given my consent yet. I've agreed to take the annex, yes, but my contract doesn't extend to shacking up with you."

She brought in the cooked food—a delicious-looking filet mignon and broth to accompany it—with a small bottle of wine.

She watched languorously, like a cat, while Hanio devoured the food.

"Is it good?" Reiko asked.

"Mmm."

"So, do you love me?" she asked in a coquettish tone.

"You cook well. You'll make someone a great wife."

"Don't be facetious. I'm being serious. I've waited so long for us to meet. You know, I even sent you a letter once. I was certain one day you'd come. I don't know why I could be so sure, but I was. You're *that person*, aren't you? The one who put a strange ad in the newspapers. The 'Life for Sale' person. Am I right?"

40

"What? Did you know that I was the person who'd put the ad in the paper when we met at the real estate agent's? How? I just happened to drop into the place as I was passing."

"I had a photo of you," Reiko replied with a nonchalant air.

"A photo? How did you get hold of it?"

"You're quite the detective, aren't you? I'm surprised someone like you is so bothered by such petit-bourgeois concerns."

She said nothing more. But whether he'd met Reiko at the real estate agent's by pure chance or not, it was clear that a photograph of him taken unawares was doing the rounds. But why, for heaven's sake? Had he unwittingly become a star in this totally unfathomable world?

After they had eaten, Reiko came and sat close to him. She took Hanio's face in her hands and peered deeply into his eyes with her own, which were frighteningly large. "So, do you want to catch my illness?"

"Mmm." Hanio gave a non-committal response.

"I'm going to lose my mind anyway. Who knows? Maybe the two of us getting together will push me right over the edge."

Reiko's words made Hanio feel a sudden pity for this young woman who had lost her chance to marry.

When Reiko took off her clothes, Hanio was startled by the beautifully translucent quality of her body. There was no sign of the ravages by drugs that he had anticipated. In the subdued lamplight, the skin enveloping that troubled and lonely spirit looked soft and unblemished. Her breasts appeared full, swelling into gentle mounds in a way that lent a feel of something archaic to her nakedness. Her waist was a little thicker than expected: her white stomach rising out of the gloom, overflowing with amiability and richness. Every point touched by Hanio's fingers sent rippling shudders through her body. This Reiko lying so quietly by his side made him think of a sorrowful, abandoned child.

At the critical moment, a furrow of pain crossed Reiko's brow, as if she were being branded. Hanio was thrown into confusion. He could hardly believe it. The sheet bore a patch of blood in the shape of a little bird.

He rolled gently away, determined to say nothing, but it was Reiko who spoke up. "So you're surprised?"

"I certainly am. That was your first time."

Reiko got up without a word and, still absolutely naked, like an odalisque, brought back some sweet wine and two liqueur glasses on a tray.

"Now I can die in peace."

"Don't be ridiculous." Hanio was feeling sleepy and his words were beginning to drift. For the moment, he had said enough about life and death.

41

Reiko started to tell him, haltingly, about herself.

She had wanted her own tomb like the one in the story. But she needed a companion to share it with, ideally someone who cherished a similar desire.

Listening to her, Hanio realized she was actually a thoughtful, shy woman, even though everything about her appearance and tone of voice suggested otherwise.

"I had made a personal resolution that I must never love anyone," she continued. "If I did fall in love, I'd only end up passing on my illness—which would be terrible. And even if I met someone, and he loved me so much that he didn't mind catching my disease, there would still be the prospect of me becoming a mental patient before long. How sad would that be? So even when someone tried it on with me, I never surrendered my body. I took Hyminal and LSD, and when I got wasted I came home. I much preferred being in the arms of my mother, who looked after me so sweetly.

"Besides, if a guy only has a few coins in his pocket, I won't look twice at him—no matter how edgy I may seem. But then again, the ones with any money are all dirty old men.

"I've wanted for so long to give my virginity to a man who was young and single, and who was willing to pay for my body, to pay for my life, to pay for the beautiful tomb I would make. I had a few other conditions, too. It would have to be someone who wouldn't regret catching my illness, someone with no thoughts for the future, someone who was willing to die with me at a moment's notice. The guy had to be willing to buy the whole package. That's why your photo struck such a chord the moment I saw it, and why I wanted to meet you."

"So how did you get to see my photo?"

"Do you mind? I was in the middle of my story. I expected more of you." Reiko was again avoiding the question.

Hanio threw out an arm and drew her disgruntled face onto his chest. He spoke to her as if he were advising a child. "Come on now. You must wake up from this foolish dream. You're still acting like a child. You're a thirty-year-old woman but you cruise around with those Shinjuku deadbeats and hold on to some selfish, hedonistic notion of painting the world blue. But that's far too simplistic. If you turn on a blue light in a tiny room, everything goes blue, but that doesn't mean you've turned the inside of the room into an ocean.

"The first thing to say is, you're not ill. That's a delusion, a self-indulgent fantasy. Secondly, you are not going to go insane. It's infantile to even consider such a crazy thing, but infantile thinking does not equal madness. Thirdly, it makes absolutely no sense for you to die merely from fear of going insane. Fourthly, no one is going to buy your life. I don't know how you can dare to ask me, a professional, to do such a thing. It's me and no one else who does the selling here. Buy your life? You must be joking. I wouldn't sink to that level.

"Listen, Reiko. People who buy other people's lives and then try to use them for their own ends are the sickos of the world. They are the lowest form of human existence. I feel nothing but pity for all my clients. But because that's the type of people they are, I've been happy to let them pay for me. But you are simply a thirty-year-old child who just lost her virginity, a woman who despairs of life because of some misguided fantasy, and who has not fathomed what it really means to be human. Nothing more than that. You don't qualify."

"But I don't want to buy your life. I want to sell my life to you."

"Don't you understand? I'm not a buyer. I'm a seller."

"Well, I'm a seller too."

"Well, you're pretty bad at it!"

"I don't pretend to be a pro."

"Looks like I'm on a winning streak, then!" Hanio said. And then the two began to laugh.

42

And so their life together began. All went well at first.

Hanio's attempts at making Reiko see things differently had no effect at all. Reiko would not let go of the belief that she was ill, destined to go mad in the near future, and she resolutely refused to be examined by a doctor.

"If I suddenly start having fits and acting insane, kill me immediately and follow me in death. Do you understand?" she would say, and other similarly wild things.

Hanio offered equivocal replies, and to all intents and purposes they spent their days in the way you might expect of a couple of lovers who had just started living together. Whenever they went out to see a film or to take a stroll, Hanio would try to rein in Reiko's hippy tastes. On their outings together, she would dress in simple, tasteful clothes, as if she were a normal young wife. The fierceness in her expression began to give way to glimmers of sophistication.

One evening, the couple were out taking a stroll in a small park in the neighborhood. They were going to view the cherry blossoms, even though many petals had been strewn about in the driving rain the previous day.

The park comprised a narrow patch of land right next to a railway track. To reach the entrance, Hanio and Reiko had to go over a raised level crossing in the road along which they had come. The cloudless sky that day meant it was hot, but the rain from the previous day had studded the ground in front of the park gate with an abundance of petals. Some sodden sheets of newspaper, battered by the rain, lay open in the earth.

In the children's play area, between the swings, horizontal bar, and jungle gym, were some enormous cherry trees, left over from a previous era. Strangely, there was no sound of children. In the completely still park, the metallic surface of the jungle gym gleamed in the evening sunlight among scattering blossoms. The couple went over to a bench. A figure perched on a swing caught their attention. He was swinging gently back and forth, the petals falling around him. A little old man sporting a neat tie.

As Hanio sat with Reiko on the bench, he observed the old man, vaguely aware of having seen him before. The man was taking peanuts from one of his pockets and popping them into his mouth with a wrinkly hand. All the while, with his other hand, he was holding up a glove puppet.

Glove puppets can be rather unwieldy, controlled by inserting an index finger inside the head cavity while the thumb and middle finger work both arms. The ones on sale in town were invariably animals, cute frogs and clowns that were geared toward children. But the puppet the old man held in his hand was clearly not for a child. It wore a rather high-class scarlet evening dress made of satin, and it boasted a pair of magnificently full breasts. Its head bore the face of a modern woman, like a mannequin, and it even wore vivid lipstick.

Holding the puppet aloft amid the fluttering petals, and chewing on his peanuts, the old man artlessly moved its head and limbs. He got the head to nod and to swing from side to side. He seemed to enjoy making it go up and down. Then he left the head to sink forward as he munched happily. The puppet appeared to be bowing in deep apology to the old man.

Hanio and Reiko were riveted, and found it hard to engage in pleasant banter, so they remained silent. Just then, two trains passed each other in opposite directions with a terrifying clatter.

The old man glanced round at the din, and suddenly noticed them. A simple, clean shirt collar went around his scrawny, desiccated neck. He twisted his head round as far as it would stretch, and locked eyes with Hanio. Immediately, the old man leapt off the swing, a look of fear on his face. The swing he'd been sitting on ricocheted off him, then crashed back, and he stepped aside, clinging with his free hand to its silvery frame.

"You're following me. I thought we had an agreement. You're actually following me."

"Not so," said Hanio. The old man was clearly terrified. "This is a total coincidence. I'm as surprised as you are."

"Really? Is that the truth?"

The old man moved away from the swing, the puppet still dangling from his hand, and approached their bench with a look of suspicion in his eyes. But the sight of Reiko sitting demurely by Hanio's side seemed to calm his nerves somewhat.

Standing in front of them, he jerked his chin toward her. "Is this lady a client?" he asked.

"No, let me introduce you to my wife. Since marrying, we've been living in this neighborhood."

Reiko gave a little bow, without saying anything.

"Well, congratulations." The old man looked bemused. "May I join you?"

"Please, feel free."

The old man sat down on the bench, the puppet on his knee. He seemed at a loss about how to get the conversation going. A hissing sound came from between his teeth.

"How can you manage hard things like peanuts with those false teeth of yours?" Hanio asked casually. The hissing brought back fond memories.

"I had these teeth specially made. Their only defect is the noise they make every time I breathe out. Do you want to see them?"

"Oh, yes please."

The old man removed the glove puppet and placed it carefully inside his jacket, then he thrust his fingers in his mouth and pulled out his teeth. What appeared to be canines jutted out long and sharp from both rows at the front, while the rear teeth were serrated like a saw.

"They look like the fangs of a vampire," Hanio said, in admiration.

The teeth were covered in bits of finely chewed peanut. The old man reinserted them.

"The canines on these teeth make eating peanuts a breeze," he explained. "And the rear teeth were made specifically in order to grind beefsteak down to nothing. You see, I'm the sort of guy who lives to eat . . . But you seem to have turned over a new leaf."

"I have you to thank for that."

"I'm amazed. There you were, in such a dangerous business . . . Now look at you. You're still alive, and married what's more. I . . . I . . ." The old man took out the puppet again and showed it to Hanio. "Look, this is Ruriko."

Hanio took the puppet in his hand. It was soft and lifeless, and the word "corpse" rose vividly to his mind. The feel of it was so creepy that he gave it back almost immediately. Upon closer inspection, it didn't really look like her, but as soon as the old man moved his hand and set the head at an angle, its face became the spitting image of Ruriko as she lay on the bed. Hanio shuddered.

"What happened to her is so sad. You must hate me now," said Hanio.

"No, not at all. I'm grateful to you. Ruriko was obviously fated to die, and it was her good fortune to meet you before she did."

Suddenly, Reiko pinched Hanio's thigh so hard he gave an involuntary start, which made the old man jump too.

"Hey, don't startle me. I can't take it. I'm too old," the old man said gloomily. "But she was amazing. Absolutely unique. She was just like these petals scattering in the setting sun: bright and showy, but cold and vain at the same time . . . Any man who slept with her could never forget her. Is it any wonder, then, that someone should have wanted to kill her? I don't think so. To hell with the law! We all live under a mountain of guilt. She didn't die by my hand. It was divine punishment, divine punishment that killed her."

The old man's ramblings seemed unlikely to come to an end. As a cue to Reiko, Hanio stood up.

"Well, we must be on our way. I won't ask for your address. And there's no point in telling you ours. Take care of yourself."

"Just a moment. Please, there's something important you should know." The old man stood up and clutched at Hanio's sweater. "If you think you can carry on selling your life, you are very much mistaken. You're being targeted. You're being monitored from afar. They'll bump you off as soon as they judge it convenient. Keep on your guard."

43

This encounter with the old man had a disturbing effect on Hanio. Until now, it had never occurred to him that his own actions were linked together like a series of interconnected rings.

He saw those times that he put his life on sale as a succession of one-off events: like throwing one bunch of flowers after another into the river. The flowers might be carried away in the water, they might sink, they might float all the way down to the sea. He never dreamt they would be gathered up and end up on display together in some vase.

That evening, a particularly tender mood pervaded the bedroom. When it was all over, Reiko's eyes were filled with a serene light.

"I think I can see myself settling down with you." Reiko was speaking from the heart.

"What? I thought you wanted this place as a nice little tomb."

"Well, I did—at first. All I was looking for was someone willing to buy my life. I guess I made such a fuss trying to find the right man that I lost myself in self-indulgent fantasies. But meeting you has been the answer to my dreams.

"I thought that people would judge me according to how much money I had, and nothing more. After all, I was a spoiled young lady with property. There was only one type suitable for me: someone willing to pay for a sick girl who came with a house. But I couldn't bear the idea of anyone doing it out of pity. The thought that someone might live and then die with me simply because they felt sympathy was anathema."

"But you're not sick."

"You're just being kind."

"I'm not being kind at all. I'm telling you the truth. You're just being silly."

"Once you find out you've been infected by me, you'll resent me for it, and that really worries me. No matter how kind you are now, the moment I go crazy you'll change your tune and toss me aside without a second thought. I can see it already. We only have this moment: now is the only time when I can enjoy the fantasy of us settling down together. I marry you, we have a child, we lead a happy, ordinary life together. That's a dream to savor. Nothing exists but the present. But until I met you, that dream had never even entered my mind."

Listening to Reiko go into the finer details of her rose-tinted fantasy, Hanio was surprised by its mediocrity.

Reiko would become a happy, loving wife. They would have one child together. The pregnancy would have a few complications, and a Caesarean birth would be required, but in the end they would produce a perfect baby boy. Of course, well before she conceived, Reiko would have stopped popping Hyminal and LSD tablets.

"Why a Caesarean?" Hanio interrupted her.

"Well, I'll be a little old for a first-time mom, so there is a high probability, don't you think?" It didn't seem to worry Reiko at all.

The comfortable tomb would be replaced by a new family home, and the tea room refurbished. The thick bushes around the house would be cut back, and the south-facing entrance cleared of most of the vegetation to allow in plenty of sunshine. *One Thousand and One Nights* would be swapped for a manual on childcare. Hanio would commute to a normal job in a company, like he used to, and a Pomeranian dog would guard the house while they were out. The traditional rock arrangement in the luxuriant garden would be replaced with a swing on a lawn. Reiko would carefully tend the flower borders around the lawn. As summer approached, she would buy an ant house for her child at the department store. These ant houses were all the rage now in the shops, and she felt she would have to buy one for the child that would never be granted to her in reality.

An ant house consisted of a small plastic container with transparent sides that revealed the coarse white sandy material packed inside. The base of the container was made of green plastic and decorated with scenes of farmhouses, woods, and hills. It had holes in every side. You inserted a few worker ants into these holes in the base, and then watched through the transparent walls as they burrowed their way through the white sand and made their nest. Everything going on inside was fully visible to the onlooker. It was a toy designed to stimulate a child's curiosity and spirit of investigation.

"It's amazing, isn't it, sweetheart?" Reiko would say to her imaginary child.

"Yes, Mama," the child would reply.

"Oh my! It's already five o'clock. Mama must put the dinner on."

"Yes, Mama."

"Now, sweetheart, you enjoy yourself alone in your playpen. All right? Daddy comes home every day at six fifteen, so I have to start cooking. When everything's bubbling away nicely, I'll hurry up and put on my makeup in time for when Daddy turns up. You'll be good, now, won't you? Be a big boy and play by yourself for a while."

"Yes, Mama . . ."

Hanio listened with a growing sense of horror to these vignettes of an imagined life that Reiko was sketching. This was nothing other than a cockroach existence! It was the embodiment of all those bugs scurrying around on a sheet of newspaper. Hadn't he opted for suicide precisely to avoid ending up like this?

Of course, Reiko's conviction that she was fatally sick was a complete illusion. But this meant she would have plenty of time to turn the life she was dreaming about into reality. So how could Hanio escape it? Little by little, and absurd as it might sound, he began to try to convince himself that Reiko really was sick: the very delusions she harbored, he reasoned, were actually symptoms of that sickness.

"But they're all pipe-dreams," Reiko would say. "I'm just letting myself fantasize because *you* are so healthy. The only thing awaiting me is insanity." She really did seem to be obsessed by his health.

Hanio was lost for words. There was something bigger going on here, he felt. Even a comfortable little tomb like this in the small hours of the night was not totally insulated from the ways of the world. Out there, restless nocturnal life continued to pulse. At the bend of the road on the nearby hill, car horns sounded sharply in the spring night, as if leaping, like the flashing fins of flying fish, from a dark viscous ocean. Useless. Useless. Useless. Is there nothing to charm us? When ten million people come together, they voice not pleasantries but profound frustration with this great city. Youngsters of the night wriggle in their multitudes like swathes of plankton. The insignificance of human life. Passion extinguished. The flavor of pleasure and anticipation lost, like gum when you chew it to death. What else can you do in the end but spit it onto the roadside? . . . Some people think that money solves everything, and they make off with public funds. Japan today is awash with such cash, and with all else that glitters. Everyone can lay their hands on money, but they're never allowed to use it for themselves. And it's the same with everything else. Succumb to temptation and make a grab at something, and you suddenly find yourself a criminal, ostracized from society. Welcome to the big city: all temptation, no satisfaction. Such was the hell that bared its fangs and whirled around Hanio and Reiko's comfortable little tomb.

Hanio's thoughts returned to more immediate matters. Could it be that Reiko was the purest, most faint-hearted, and most ordinary of young women, and she had simply hit upon this elaborate ruse as an act of self-preservation?

Reiko, still eager to play the role of the devoted wife, got up from bed and slipped on a negligee. "Will you have a nightcap?" she asked.

"Good idea. Something sweet would be good. How about some cherry liqueur?"

"I think I'll join you."

She went to the corner cabinet, took out a couple of liqueur glasses, and poured out the drinks. She returned carrying a silver tray on which were set the glasses filled with the dark red liquid.

"Bottoms up." Reiko spoke tenderly, and with a certain audacity in her smile. They clinked glasses and put them to their lips.

But just as he was about to take a sip, Hanio noticed a slight trembling in Reiko's fingers. He quickly knocked the glass out of her hand. The liqueur in her glass spilled onto the silver tray, covering it in dark red.

Hanio took a sniff of his own drink, then emptied its contents likewise onto the tray, now suddenly awash with red liquid.

"How could you do such a thing!" Hanio shook Reiko's shoulders angrily.

"But surely you understand. I just thought that now would be the best moment. To die together." Reiko sank to the floor, weeping.

"This is not what I wanted," said Hanio.

Hanio felt his heart beating, even faster than when he faced death on previous occasions. He confronted her, arms folded.

"Coward!" she said. "Your life was supposed to be for sale. Why have you changed your mind?"

"You're getting things confused here. I don't recall ever selling my life to you. But the main point is, I was paying you!"

"You just don't want to die with me, do you?"

"That's enough of your sob story. Pathetic! If you're that keen to give up your life, at least show a bit more backbone. But whatever you decide, my life is my own affair. I'm quite prepared to sell my life as long as it's my decision. But when some selfish so-and-so messes me about, and then even tries to poison me while I'm not looking, I'm not prepared to take it. You've misjudged me. I'm not that kind of guy."

"Well, what kind of guy are you, then?"

Hanio was stumped. The truth is, he was not sure what kind of guy he was. The angry, puffed-up words he'd just come out with hung in the air like balloons. Until that moment, he simply could not have imagined such thoughts issuing from his own mouth. There had to be some rationale to the way he had spoken, but he couldn't quite make sense of it. Maybe it did all boil down to the fact that, actually, he didn't want to die.

But did that mean he was betraying everything he had come to believe in? Death is death, isn't it, whether you put your life up for sale, or someone else does the job for you? He might make a big fuss about acting according to his "own will," but surely the reason he'd set up his "Life for Sale" business in the first place was that, having failed to take his own life, he was hoping for the chance to die by the hand of another. He had certainly not started the business from a desire to earn money. And yet here he was being showered with money by all his clients . . . In which case, perhaps the most desirable way for him to lose his life was as a sudden event, exactly like Reiko had attempted. Maybe the death that Reiko had been plotting simply proved that she was indeed an eminently suitable, kind, and gentle woman, with the purest of intentions!

His thoughts continued to race, and his heart to pound. Was that fear he was feeling? From now on, Hanio could not afford to let down his defenses.

44

The matter was put to rest for that evening, but thereafter relations with Reiko became extremely strained. He now felt wary whenever she offered him anything to eat or drink.

"There's no poison in it," Reiko would say, teasingly. "I already tested it."

She had become very wary that Hanio might try to run away. Even as she joked about poison, there was pure toxicity in the mere look of her eyes. The woman who had once spoken of gentle childlike things was nowhere to be seen. Her every word was laced with contempt:

"Nothing matters more than your precious life, does it? What if you caught a cold? It would be a complete disaster . . .

"Well, I guess I'll just have to let you live to a ripe old age . . .

"I wonder if I should get a Pomeranian dog? I don't feel safe somehow. If anything happened, you certainly wouldn't be the knight in shining armor to come and rescue me . . .

"You're a bundle of nerves every time we have a meal! It's unbearable. Maybe I should stir something extra 'nutritious' into your food . . ."

Whenever he left the house, she would accompany him. And every time she went out, he would be dragged along.

Reiko began to abuse sleeping pills. Her taste in fashion became ever more outlandish, and she devised one eccentric outfit after another. Taking her cue from paper lanterns, she created a paper dress that stuck out around her in a lantern shape. She would take Hanio out to dance at go-go bars and once, when the dancing was in full flow, she called out: "I'm a paper lantern. I'm full of fire inside. Rip me up. Rip me up, I say!" The boys tore off her lantern outfit, and she did a crazy dance dressed in nothing but a bright red petticoat.

When she was outrageously high, Hanio would look for an opportunity to escape, but this was precisely the time when her intuition became exceptionally acute. "Where are you off to?" She would stand firmly in his way. Even when he went to the toilet, she would be waiting outside the door. As Reiko had noted previously, drugs gave her the ability to have premonitions and predict how things would turn out. "You're going to try and make a getaway tonight, aren't you? Well, I'm not gonna let you go. I know perfectly well you've sewn all your bank savings into your waistband so you can make off at any time. You keep it on, even when you're in bed. Coward! Thinking of nothing but yourself all the time."

As they danced to the frantic disco beat, she would continue to bawl right into Hanio's face.

"Cheapskate! If you try to leave me I'll kill you, so if you want to live, you'd better stay right where you are. So what do you think? I've finally gone insane, haven't I? I never realized how much fun insanity would be. But now I do, I wish I'd gone mad earlier."

One particular evening at the disco, Reiko asked him to accompany her to the ladies' room—she did not feel at all well.

He could hardly refuse, but then another female customer made a fuss and complained to management. The manager took him by the neck and threw him out.

This was Hanio's last chance!

Like a shot, he took off into the dark streets. He made a point of sticking to the maze of little alleyways, doing his best to follow an unpredictable route. Running would raise suspicions, and there were few taxis around at that time. He feared it would take too long to get bogged down in negotiations with a taxi driver, so his only option was to keep walking, and not to stop.

Every moment was fraught with danger. In his desperation to find a place of safety, he followed any road that presented itself. He lost himself in one house-lined street after another, passed from one bright neon-lit alley to the next, stepped on the bodies of sewer rats, and pushed aside streetwalkers who tugged at his sleeve.

Suddenly he emerged into a dark, dismal section of the city in which quiet houses with low eaves huddled together under a railway bridge. Mounds of rubbish lined the embankment. The road was unpaved. In the gloom he could make out the scattered forms of large stones left behind after construction work.

Hanio suddenly realized that he'd been concentrating on nothing else but walking. Wiping his sweaty forehead with a handkerchief, he slowed his pace a little and was about to turn into a side street when he became aware of someone stealthily pursuing him. The footsteps picked up when Hanio increased his pace, and stopped when he stopped.

45

He glanced back, but could see no one. Yet when he walked faster, the footsteps still pursued him.

Hanio thought it through. Perhaps it was his own footsteps that unsettled him. He decided to ignore them. A little further on he saw he was approaching a brightly lit shopping street. He had chosen to stick to dark areas, but now he was desperate to come out into the light. He quickened his pace but suddenly felt a sharp sting in his thigh.

That couldn't be a mosquito bite—not at this time of the year. The pain ceased immediately, so he pressed forward and finally emerged, with some relief, into the broad, well-lit road.

Naturally, the shops were all closed. It was the usual kind of street with a brilliantly lit archway over the road, shop signs and display windows illuminated for no one's benefit, and a cacophony of traffic.

Just before an alley on the opposite side, Hanio saw a paper lantern advertising the presence of a hotel in white lettering:

Stay: 850 yen
Rest: 300 yen

Making sure that the coast was clear, he crossed the road, checked again, and entered the alley.

The Merciful Light Inn, a small establishment, was clearly a love hotel. How this solitary establishment had ended up in a place like this, he had no idea. In the entrance was a dim spherical light, covered with insects, whose very bodies as they clustered around it spoke of the ephemeral. He opened the glass door, but there was no one at reception.

A sign read: "If no one available, please ring bell." Under it was the cracked yellow button. Hanio pressed. He heard a soft ringing somewhere within the building. Then, moments later, the sound of someone stumbling, dropping something, and muttering. A bout of coughing. A tiny old woman appeared.

"So, you want an all-night stay?" She stared right at him with her beady eyes.

"Yes. Is there a room available?" Hanio knew the answer would be yes, but he made a show of being polite.

"None of the good ones, unfortunately. We do a roaring trade here, despite the downturn in the economy. We offer only basic amenities, no air-conditioning or anything like that, yet still the customers come, even in high summer. I suppose we're a bit out of the way, so people feel at ease. It's the same attitude people have toward a pawnbroker's."

Hanio understood instantly that the hotel offered peep shows. From the way she had so pointedly mentioned "good rooms," he was sure she was angling to squeeze five thousand yen out of him and lead him to a booth with a little peephole. Well, she was good with words, he had to give her that. The way she hinted at the special service they provided—by suggesting they could still pull in customers during summer, even without air-conditioning—was a stroke of genius.

Hanio was curt. "A bad room will do. So, that'll be eight hundred for the night?"

Her expression hardened discernibly, as if a door had been closed. She led him up to a tiny, cupboard-like room toward the rear of the first floor and took the eight hundred yen. "You'll find the mattress and bedding inside the cupboard. Lay it out when you want to sleep."

With that, she turned and descended the creaking stairs. It didn't look as though he would be getting any tea.

Exhausted, longing to lie down, Hanio wondered if he should ask her politely to lay out the bed. But the very thought of those beady eyes stopped him.

The small, narrow room shook with the vibration of the traffic, so loud that it seemed almost to be inside the hotel. He listened to the roaring sea that was the city at night. Down the corridor, a woman cried out. But her cries were followed by a succession of silken moans, so Hanio decided not to concern himself about it. He caught a faint smell of the toilet.

On the other side of this ceiling was a starry sky enveloped in smog. As Hanio lay with arm on pillow and looking up at the rain-blotched ceiling, he sensed the design of the Almighty. The same vast starry sky that hung over the ceiling of a great convention hall, replete with glittering chandeliers, also hung over the ceiling of this dismal, gray hotel. Beneath the sky, wretched loneliness was no jot better or worse than good fortune and success. To put it another way, wherever you stood, the same starry sky was peering down. He knew that to be true. And that was precisely the reason why the meaninglessness of his own life connected directly with the starry sky. Hidden away in this flophouse, Hanio had become, you might say, a "prince of stars."

He pulled the musty mattress from the cupboard, and laid it on the floor. He had a strong urge to lie down just as he was, but he felt the need at least to get out of his trousers, so he quickly yanked them off. Hanio felt a smart pain shoot through his thigh. A tiny splinter seemed to have lodged in his skin, through his trousers. But he couldn't locate it. Using the light of the lamp, he finally spied a broken fragment of the splinter buried darkly in his skin. There was no blood but it ached a little.

Try as he might, he found it impossible to sleep. He kept being assailed by a vision of Reiko's face staring right at him, her hands groping around inside an ant house. She picked out two or three ants and sprinkled them on his face. The dull pain in his thigh seemed to have made him feverish. His entire thigh felt hot and heavy, and a good night's sleep eluded him all the more.

46

He checked out of the Merciful Light Inn early next morning, and dragged his aching leg around in search of a pharmacy already open for business. The store that he found gave him ointment and antibiotics without even requiring to view his wound. Hanio applied a quick dressing in a nearby coffee shop. He felt a little lighter in himself.

It struck him that, in view of the circumstances, the best way to avoid detection was probably to live as a wealthy guest in a big hotel. He decided he should purchase some luxury travel bags and presentable ready-made clothes. All he had to do was to wait for the bank to open.

When he got into his room in the K— Hotel, it was nearly midday. The room had a nice outlook and he stretched out on the soft double bed, hoping to recover from the previous night's lack of sleep. The leg pain seemed to have improved a little. Thinking he might apply more ointment, he examined his thigh in the light coming through the window.

It was a beautiful May day. A light scattering of clouds could been seen over the motorway, along which a stream of cars—Minis mostly, by the look of things—sped quietly. Finally, he was able to step back a little and see things more clearly. His absurd delusion that someone was after him was due to Reiko.

But then, a single thought came back and would not let go: that photo Reiko said she saw. Where did it come from? Why would a portrait of him get passed around?

The fact that such a matter even bothered Hanio surely proved that life was dear to him. Why should anything worry him if he had no concern for his life? But was refusing to put his own death in the hands of another really the same as being attached to life?

Quietly, in the bright light, Hanio examined his naked thigh close up. He wiped away the remnants of the ointment, and scrutinized what was left of the splinter. For a splinter, it had a strangely precise shape. Its blackness was more reminiscent of wire than dark woody fiber. It seemed thicker and more of a spindle shape than he remembered. It had gone in quite deeply, apparently. No wonder it was festering.

He racked his brains, but could not think how he might have picked the splinter up. During his attempt to avoid those footsteps, he had hidden himself among garbage bins. Maybe he'd been pierced by some wire at that point? No, it almost certainly had to have been while he was walking. But how odd to get a splinter just then. On further thought, he seemed to remember hearing a whooshing sound like a shuttlecock cutting through the air when the splinter pierced him. But he couldn't be sure now if he'd imagined it.

Hanio burst out laughing. Here he was, worrying himself to the bone: what a complete neurotic he had become! And yet he had not felt the slightest concern when the blood was being sucked out of him every day by the vampire woman!

Come to think of it, he remembered something he had learned long ago, but had subsequently forgotten—that living and worrying were one and the same thing. Perhaps this was evidence that he had got his "life" back, and he just hadn't realized it until now.

"If the wound gets worse, I'll see a doctor," he promised himself.

He applied some ointment, took his antibiotics, and eventually fell into a pleasant sleep.

When he awoke, it was dark all around him. He was hungry and about to go down to the restaurant, but the thought of drawing any attention put him off the idea. He was afraid of something, that was for sure. He could just see himself going out there, on show to all and sundry: he worried about his fear becoming public. Why not have his meal in his room, without fear and just the way he liked it? He wouldn't have to worry about others. And he had money to spare.

He used room service to order a tenderloin steak, a Waldorf salad, and a bottle of wine. When he saw the steward enter his room, pushing his creaky cart, Hanio couldn't help stealing a look at his face.

Tall, and probably rather snooty, the steward had clearly just spent a lot of effort squeezing blackheads. But his unprepossessing appearance was no proof that he was unconnected to any organization. Everyone affiliated to an organization conspires to kill those who exist in complete isolation.

The meal and wine were delightful. He watched television until late, but then found it really hard to get to sleep. His afternoon doze came back to curse him. Staring at the gray, flickering static on the TV once the programs had run their course, he got a sudden premonition that the face of Ruriko, or Reiko, or the vampire woman was going suddenly to emerge and start talking to him. But the flickering gray sand on the screen never changed.

Around two in the morning, finally a yawn. This encouraged him to go to bed but, just as he was on his way to the bathroom, there was a discreet knock at the door.

A client, Hanio thought immediately. But how could a client find a way here to purchase his life? For one thing, he'd canceled the newspaper ad ages ago. And he'd checked in under an alias, so how would anyone know his whereabouts?

Who was it, then?

Another knock, this time a bit louder. Hanio took the plunge and threw open the door. In the corridor was a man in a raincoat and a felt hat.

"Who are you?" Hanio said.

"Are you Mr. Tanaka?" the man asked. He had a thick, viscous voice.

"No, I'm not."

"Sorry to have troubled you."

But there was a toneless quality to his voice. In fact, he did not seem the least bit sorry. Hanio watched as the man turned on his heel and went off down the corridor. Once he'd shut the door, he could feel his heart racing.

"Why ask the question and then just walk off? There's something fishy going on. They must have tracked me down. I need to move to another hotel tomorrow."

Brooding, he locked the door and got ready for bed. But there was no way he could sleep now.

The pain in his leg was bothering him less. But he couldn't get out of his head the thought that the man might be loitering in the corridor outside his room. How fearless, utterly fearless he had felt when he first put his life up for sale! But now, a warm furry fear clung to his chest, digging its claws right in. Like lying in bed with a cat in his arms.

47

Hanio checked out first thing next morning, carrying nothing but an empty bag, and hid himself in another major hotel. He had no urge to go into town, so he lolled around all day in front of the TV. With no exercise, he didn't even get hungry.

As night deepened and the hotel became quieter, anxiety settled thickly on his mind. He wanted to flee but no matter how far he fled, he felt certain that those unaccountable footsteps would come in pursuit.

For the first time in a long while, Hanio felt a sense of

anticipation. In the past, when waiting for clients to turn up and buy his life, he would put aside all normal concerns with time and regular life, and remain untroubled. But now, he was feeling anxious about something he could not quite put his finger on: it was like dealing with a new lover. He had never before sensed that the future might embody something important and substantial.

Two in the morning. The corridor could well have belonged to a hospital, leading to a morgue. He opened the door a crack and peered out to make sure it was clear. A solitary red leather chair opposite the elevator gleamed dully under a sconce.

It came as no surprise when, at two thirty, there was another knock on the door. And, when Hanio failed to answer, another knock. After much hesitation, Hanio finally opened the door. A short, stout man in a striped suit stood before him. A different man from the one the previous night.

"Who are you?"

"Are you Mr. Ueno?"

"No, I'm not."

"Sorry to have troubled you." The man bowed politely and walked off calmly in the direction of the elevator.

Hanio locked the door and returned to bed. His chest was pounding. Just then, pain ran through his thigh again. Hanio had a sudden flash of inspiration.

"Of course! Damn! That's what it is."

Using the lamplight to locate his wound, he wiped it clean of ointment and touched it with his finger. Then, bending his body, he placed his ear against it. An almost imperceptible vibration was coming from the black splinter left in him. Someone had fired an exquisitely small mini-transceiver into his thigh. Which meant that, wherever he fled, they would find him.

He made an attempt to gouge it out with his nails, but it was too deeply embedded. He took a moment then to work out a strategy.

"OK, maybe I shouldn't try to remove it now. Clearly it's already sent a signal to my adversaries saying where I am—that's why they came to check. I should take it out when I leave in the morning, and then go to ground. No doubt I'll need to go to the hospital, but I'd rather that than have it taken out by a doctor and blow my cover, I'll do it myself and get treated afterward."

Sleep came easily to him once he'd worked out his plan. The ordinary knife that arrived at his room with breakfast the next morning was not up to the job, he decided, so he ordered a steak despite having no appetite for it. Hanio heated the steak knife's sharp blade with the flame of a match, then dug it into his own thigh.

He stuck the blade in, gave it a flick up, and a tiny steel wire popped out along with a gush of blood.

48

The doctor examined the wound in Hanio's thigh and frowned. He was young with a self-confident manner and a long nose that gave him a supercilious look.

"How on earth did you get this wound? It looks like the flesh has been gouged out with a sharp tool. If this was done in a fight, I need to report it to the police."

"You're right. My flesh has been gouged out. But I did it myself."

"So what happened?"

"I caught my leg on a rusty old nail. I was worried I might get tetanus."

"A bit of an overreaction, I would say . . . You amateurs . . ."

The doctor asked nothing more. He lined up the sutures, then injected Hanio with a local anesthetic. The injection was painful, but the thought that "they" would have no idea of where he was provided an indescribable sense of relief. This place was all white walls, shelves lined with scalpels, and metal basins full of antiseptic, without a shred of comfort on offer. But the certainty that his whereabouts were unknown was comfort enough.

Hanio closed his eyes. The pain had gone completely. The sensation was as if someone were stitching together two stiff pieces of leather over his wounded thigh.

He left with instructions to return one week later to have the stitches removed. It was unlikely that he would come back here, he thought. He could drop into any old clinic to get the job done.

As might be expected, Hanio kept to the shadows under the eaves. It was a new habit for him. Whenever he emerged into the light, he would keep a lookout for anyone tailing him. He took particular care at corners.

Where should he go?

First thing was to get out of Tokyo. No use lying to himself anymore. It was the fear of death that was driving him now.

49

Nothing is safer than not even knowing your destination yourself.

The anesthetic was wearing off. He dragged his aching leg as far as Ikebukuro, and then looked around various counters in S— department store. The menswear fashions, shirts, the fridges, rattan blinds, fans, and air conditioners all suggested that, even before the June rainy season had begun, spring had had its day and it was already almost summer. The huge number of products spoke of compact little families, in their compact little houses, where these goods would ultimately end up. The thought almost suffocated him. Why are people so desperate to live? Isn't it unnatural that people who have not even been exposed to the danger of death should feel a desire to live? It was only people like himself who should have the right to cherish such a desire.

Boarding a Seibu Line train with no destination in mind, Hanio found himself captivated by the view of fields in the suburbs. He had the odd feeling that the passengers were all pretending not to know him even though they did. A young man who looked like a member of some radical students' group, a schoolgirl dressed in a beautiful traditional kimono, a middle-aged man with a square-set physique who looked as if he might once have served as a noncommissioned army officer: there they stood, hanging on to their straps, stealing looks at him. They might have been checking portraits of criminals on "Wanted" posters you find pasted up in front of a police station.

"That's him there. I'll pretend not to notice now, but I'll inform the station staff later when I get off at the next stop."

They seemed to have detected in Hanio's face the hint of an enmity toward society.

The warm air of May mingled with the odor of people's bodies in the carriage, bringing home to him for the first time in ages the unbearable smell of communal living. He wanted to live, that was now certain. But could someone who had once managed to escape society's clutches find the courage to commit himself again to that pungent stench? Society operates smoothly precisely because people remain unaware of their own smell. The student's stinking socks that haven't been washed in a week, the sweet underarm odor of a schoolgirl, and her distinctively world-weary "virginal scent," the middle-aged man who reeks like a chimney covered in soot. People never hold back when it comes to giving off their own scents. Hanio liked to think he produced no smell or odor, but he could not be certain.

He bought a ticket to Hannō, which was the end of the line, so he could alight wherever the fancy took him, but he became anxious again that someone might be following him. He suspected that, if he were suddenly to make a show of getting off at a station, someone would come hurrying after him. To test this out, he made a dash to the doors a second before they were about to close.

But he stopped in his tracks, without getting off. A thin man sporting a wispy beard had been trying to scramble off behind him but, his way suddenly blocked, he missed his chance and the doors closed in his face. All the way to the next station, the man stared hard and long at Hanio. Though Hanio found this very annoying, he took great comfort in the fact that he was being stared at with such naked animosity.

At Hannō, Hanio was relieved when the passengers who got off with him all went their own separate ways. He walked to the quiet square in front of the station where he noticed a large map displaying hiking routes. He was too exhausted even to think about any more walking, however.

Not far away from him was a seedy-looking inn. All Hanio had to do was to stand at the entrance in his smart clothes for them to come out and guide him to a room.

He opened the round window in the room and whiled away the time gazing at the sky until the evening. What a flat, thoroughly matter-of-fact town Hannō was! The blueness of the sky quietly faded as evening encroached. And then he noticed a spider dropping down rapidly from the top of the window.

The spider stopped in front of Hanio's eyes, its single thread of silk glittering in the evening light.

The spider was tiny. It was hard to make out clearly, but what looked like a black scrap of yarn rolled into a ball dangled from the end of the thread. The ball reminded him of silkworm gut. The sight was unpleasant, but Hanio couldn't tear his eyes away. The spider started to sway on its thread, back and forth, as if it had decided to put on a circus display.

Think you can impress me? Hanio thought, idly.

Next moment, the swinging grew violent, and the spider began to grow in size before his eyes. It also seemed to be changing into something else. It was now an axe with a sharp blade. The thread turned into a thick, sparkling, silvery web. The axe made a cutting sound through the air, aiming straight for Hanio's face. There was a white glint to its blade.

Hanio fell back onto the tatami floor, his hands covering his face. When he came to, there was no sign of the spider: a faint three-day moon floated in the center of the round window. Perhaps he had mistaken the crescent moon for the blade of an axe.

"They're even screwing with my head!"

Terrified, he suddenly recalled Reiko's illness.

50

But after that, nothing happened.

Hanio went out several times to get to know his new neighborhood, but there was really nothing worth seeing in the streets. A manufacturer of wooden bathtubs, an old-fashioned confectioner's shop with overhanging eaves, on a wide road whose beauty had otherwise been destroyed by extensive redevelopment. Row after row of insignificant homes surrounded by hedges. It looked like the sort of town inhabited by truly apathetic people. Surprisingly, he found that comforting.

One evening, he was strolling through one of these completely deserted parts of town. He approached a small raised level crossing in the road when a truck suddenly came hurtling toward him across the track.

As it came his way it looked menacingly huge, but Hanio found himself gazing at it with a sense of awe. Framed against the dusty evening sky, it reminded him of one of those kabuto helmets worn by savage tribes in ancient times.

The truck bounced over the track and came straight toward him as he stood on the wide, empty road. Was this a bad dream? he thought, and jumped out of its way. He fled to the other side of the road, but the truck turned toward him. There were no shops around into which he could dive and seek assistance: just long, expressionless lines of hedges and modest wooden fences. Whether he fled to the left or right, the truck pursued him, as if hunting a human just for the fun of it. He could see the faint reflection of clouds in the windshield inundated with evening sky. It was impossible to make out the driver's face.

Without waiting to read the license plate, Hanio escaped into a little lane that branched off the road. Surely, the truck would not be able to follow him up here? He slowed down, and gradually edged further into the narrow lane.

But the truck still pursued him. Hanio found himself trapped against an old, stone-pillared gateway with its doors firmly shut. There was no way out: the truck pressed up to him, to within an inch of his nose. Then suddenly it went into reverse, and withdrew from the lane like a steely black roiling wave.

Hanio's heart beat crazily, and he had to crouch down. That time when he collapsed with anemia while walking with the vampire, he had experienced the most exquisite sense of loss, but this was different: a terror that he had never tasted before.

51

Hanio did not want to go back to his inn: their dinners were nothing to get excited about. Not even Hannō offered a safe haven for him.

After making sure the truck had truly disappeared, Hanio decided to venture into the brightly lit shopping arcade, so he cautiously stepped back onto the broad, dusty, excessively manicured streets. But now lots of people seemed to be walking around—where could they have come from?—and this actually made him feel even more uneasy.

To describe it as a shopping arcade was stretching it. It was little more than a series of shops on the outskirts of town. One particularly soulless store had a dingy display window filled with nothing but great mounds of sports shoes. The countless shoes looked as if they had been collected from deceased inmates of an internment camp. They were crushed out of shape, with their rubber soles and limp, dangling laces pressed against the glass. There were piles and piles of them.

It wasn't all bad. Street lamps dotted the whole town, and crowds of people gathered before brightly lit shops selling fresh vegetables and fish.

Hanio heard a familiar old humming: it sounded like a honeybee. It was musical, it had warmth, and it conveyed an indescribable hint of nostalgia. The sound was emanating from a small sawmill workshop. Through the half-open door, he could see brightly colored wood shavings and the faint gleam of a round electric saw. On the wooden door was a sign:

From small boxes to bookshelves
Woodwork products made to order on the spot

He gave it a brief thought, then moved on to a watch shop. There was absolutely nothing chic or modern about this place—it was the sort of shop that belonged to a completely bygone age. Hanio entered without hesitating.

"I'm looking for a watch."

"Of course. We're a watch shop after all. What kind are you looking for?" A woman, evidently the owner, had come out. She had a white, puffy face.

"I'd like to buy a stopwatch. The loudest one you have."

"Let me check our stock . . ."

Hanio purchased a traditional old stopwatch: it would not have been out of place at a Meiji-era sporting event. He did not recognize the manufacturer. When he pressed the button on top, the second hand gave off a steady, jarringly assertive sound.

With his newly acquired purchase, he went back to the sawmill he had seen earlier.

"Would you be able to make a small box? I need it right away."

"No problem. You've caught me at a good moment," replied the thin, rather age-worn man, the very image of a carpenter, without even looking up.

"Please make me a box for this stopwatch. It's extremely urgent."

"Wait. Is it a gift box you're thinking of? They ought to have had one of those at the watch shop."

"No, I want a special kind of box. One that doesn't give any indication of what's inside. A big one, please, in as simple a style as you can make it. I don't want it to reveal any part of the watch face or anything else that might give it away."

"So you're not actually interested in it as a watch?"

"Please, no questions. Just follow my instructions. I want you to leave only the button on top of the watch sticking out through a hole. Everything else should be covered. Then paint the whole box with black lacquer."

"So the watch itself doesn't have to be visible?"

"That's right. I'm interested only in the sound," Hanio explained patiently.

The man proceeded to knock up a rough and ready box, into which the stopwatch was fitted, the button sticking out through a small hole. Black lacquer was then slapped over the coarse-grained wood. It was impossible to tell what it held, but when you pushed the button a distinct tick-tock could be felt vibrating against the sides.

"At last. A defensive weapon," Hanio whispered to himself.

It was rather bulky to insert into his jacket pocket, but Hanio put it there nevertheless, feeling a little easier now that he had it. Whenever he pressed the button, he would feel the second hand start to make that emphatic ticking sound in his pocket.

"Even if I come to a place like this, in the back of beyond, they'll sniff me out. There's no getting away from them."

Hanio had determined it was time to stop running. It was not that he had lost all sense of fear, but the days passed without incident. Every morning when he awoke, it felt wonderful to still be alive. And he was relieved that those spider fantasies never reappeared.

Now, hikers often passed in front of Hannō Station, but it was rare to see one from overseas. One day when Hanio went to the station to buy some cigarettes, a refined, white-haired foreigner in his forties politely removed his green Tyrolean hat and asked him for directions. He was dressed in plaid knickerbockers.

"Could you possibly tell me where Mount Rakan is?"

"Mount Rakan? Go past the Chamber of Commerce and turn right. When you get to the police station, take a left. Once you've passed the town hall, Mount Rakan should come into view." He was already giving directions like a local.

"I see. Thank you. Look, I'm terribly sorry, but I'd be so grateful if you could accompany me, at least till I get my bearings. I'm hopeless with directions. I'd really appreciate it."

With nothing else to occupy him, Hanio decided to act as guide to this affable-looking gentleman.

The foreigner looked up at the sky: "Good feather, isn't it?"

"I think you mean 'weather.'" Hanio's bonhomie even extended to correcting his words.

The side of the Chamber of Commerce was in shade at this time of day, and two or three cars were parked by it. One of them was black, clearly a foreign car, and beautifully polished.

"What a great car!" The foreigner seemed at first just to caress it as he passed by, but then, casually, he opened one of the back doors. Hanio couldn't believe his eyes.

"Get in," the foreigner ordered in a low, rough voice. He held a pistol in his hand.

52

As the car sped off, Hanio was still having his hands cuffed and a pair of sunglasses thrust over his eyes.

The sunglasses were stylish. They were fitted with small, triangular lenses on either side which should have meant that even when you looked sideways you still saw through darkened glass. But Hanio could see nothing. Despite their ordinary appearance, these sunglasses were painted with mercury on the inside. In effect, Hanio had been blindfolded. No doubt this was to keep him ignorant of the destination.

The man in the Alpine hat was at the steering wheel. But he

and Hanio were not alone. As soon as Hanio was bundled into the back, another man had sat up abruptly and stuck the glasses on him. The man now held the muzzle of a gun pressed into his side. Hanio hadn't had time to take in his facial features.

There was silence as the car drove along. Where will I be killed? Hanio wondered. Some light jazz on the car radio was all he could hear. He found it very difficult to gather together any real thoughts.

The moment he'd put out that "Life for Sale" ad, he had already sealed his own fate: a violent death. No getting away from it. This unadulterated, raw realization cut through him like searing heartburn. And yet, to his surprise, the fear he'd felt while on the run had suddenly receded.

What exactly was the fear of death? All the time Hanio had felt pursued by death, his eyes were etched with nothing but fear, no matter how many times he'd tried to look away. Fear had been like a strange black chimney rising high up on the horizon. But now, that chimney had disappeared from sight.

Once he'd had his stitches removed at a surgery in Hannō, the pain in his thigh had completely disappeared, but he still remembered what a source of worry that pain had been. People tend to be most terrified by the inexplicable. Fear seems to fade when a possible solution arises.

The man checked Hanio's hands several times over, as if he were nervous about whether they were securely handcuffed. Hanio could tell from the hairy knuckles that the man was a foreigner. He was also aware of the body odor emanating through his clothes. A gaseous smell, redolent of chives, but somehow powerfully sweet. It could only belong to a Westerner.

At first Hanio intended to calculate calmly the number of times the car turned left, the point at which it emerged onto asphalt-covered roads, and the number of level crossings it passed, but he soon realized that such an exercise was futile. If the drive had been short he could have mustered a guess, but the car kept going for more than two hours. Considering how many paved roads they took during that period, it did not seem particularly likely that they were planning to take him deep into the mountains, shoot him dead, and dispose of his body at the bottom of a ravine. They might well be on their way to Tokyo.

After some time, the car ran along a bumpy road, making it roll badly from side to side, and then went up a rather steep incline. He could feel that the wind had picked up. It was growing dark.

When the car finally came to a halt, he became aware that the anxiety he felt was less about being killed and more about how long they would keep him waiting before they did so.

Hanio was made to get out of the car, walk along a graveled path, and enter a house. He felt carpet under his feet: a sure sign that the house was a Western one.

53

Hanio seemed to be in a basement room. The room had a cold, bare, concrete floor, and they made him sit down on a chair, hands bound in front of him. The chair was one of several that were placed in a row in front of a simple table. His dark glasses were removed.

Six men were in the room with him, counting the two who had ridden with him in the car. The other four were all people he recognized. Three were the Westerners present at the drug experiment using beetle extract—today, the elderly Henry was without his dachshund. The fourth was that middle-aged, shady Asian man, Ruriko's patron, wearing that unforgettable beret.

He looked just like he did before, even to the point of carrying a large sketchbook.

The man, complete with comical beret, offered Hanio a cigarette and then was good enough to light it for him. He sat himself down in the next chair. The other men, some sitting on chairs, some standing, all looked hard at Hanio. The two who had been his companions in the car had guns pointed toward him as if ready to fire at a moment's notice.

"Right, let's start the interrogation." The Asian spoke in a strangely warm drawl, which reverberated deeply. "First, I would appreciate it if you were to confess here and now that you are a police officer."

Hanio was dumbfounded. This was the last thing he expected. "How can I be a police officer?"

"Look, you can use all the fancy words you like. One way or another, you'll end up confessing it. Do you get me? OK, I think the quickest way is probably for me to explain why we haven't disposed of you until now but left you to your own devices. So that's where I'll begin. I prefer persuasive, peaceful methods. I leave the killing to others.

"When your 'Life for Sale' advertisement first came out in the newspaper, I thought it was fishy, so I got an old man, one of our stooges, to go to your place. I should introduce him to you. He's been dying to meet you too." He clapped his hands, creating a sound that made the whole room resound like thunder. "Come on, where are you?"

An old man came into the room through a second door. He acknowledged Hanio with a silent nod from a distance, making a hissing sound through his teeth.

"My apologies," he said.

This polite tone seemed to irritate the Asian. "That's enough of that. Still, tonight I'm looking forward to sketching our young Hanio as he meets his end. That's why I've brought my sketchbook with me. I want to draw you in various positions, so I'm hoping you'll adopt all sorts of poses as you die, writhing about in excruciating pain. I'm sure you can understand where I'm coming from.

"The ad that you posted came to our attention because we had become aware that our organization was the object of a secret police investigation—even though we knew very little beyond that basic fact. We were naturally drawn to you because we thought we might have a chance of getting to the bottom of it all if we used someone like you: working undercover, and apparently with so little regard for yourself that you were willing to put out a weird ad like that.

"So we first put you together with Ruriko. Ruriko already knew too much about the organization. The way things were, we couldn't be sure how much she might spill the beans to other people about the ACS. That's why we intended to bump her off at the earliest opportunity. So once we'd introduced her to you, we got rid of her. We thought that would definitely get you to make contact with your colleagues in the police.

"But you didn't fall for it! We couldn't believe how smart you were! You were too cautious for our liking. By allowing you to return home alive after your visit to her, our intention was to get a sense of how you gathered information and made your reports. We had of course taken a secret photograph of your face. Here. This sketchbook doubles as a camera. Take a look."

The man showed Hanio. The cover had a stylish design with the two O's in the word SKETCHBOOK as two eyes, one wide open, the other shut. In the center of the open eye was a lens. The cover was awfully thick, it had to be said.

"But you played dumb and made no contact at all with the police. We began to wonder what you were up to that time you had dinner with the stuffed mouse. But we checked it out later, and failed to find any transmitter inside it. The skill with which you avoided giving yourself away was quite masterful. Amazing.

"We then decided to use a second woman—another one of our stooges. We'd pinned our hopes on her, expecting her to use all her wiles to extract the truth out of you. But then the old bag managed to fall head over heels in love with you instead, and got herself wasted instead of you.

"It's always a bit of a problem, how to dispose of the corpses, but with suicides it can be a little easier. After consultation with Henry here and the other guys, we decided to let you go once more and give you a bit more space to play around in. Sooner or later, we knew we'd have to bump you off, but for now we wanted you to act as a decoy to lure some more police spies into our trap. But you were ever the clever guy. You never let down your guard.

"And then you went and hitched up with that vampire woman. At that point, we were on the verge of deciding that you must just be a complete wacko, with some kind of a death wish, and that we'd obviously been mistaken. The whole thing had become so absurd, we could only hope that the vampire woman would suck you dry of blood as soon as possible and finish you off that way. That would have suited us down to a tee.

"But that's not what happened, is it? You really put your life on the line going under cover as deeply as that. What a stellar spy you are!

"And then, what did you do? We know exactly, don't we? You made a brilliant show of suffering from dizzy fits due to anemia so you could get yourself admitted to the hospital. And while you were in there, we relaxed and slackened our surveillance, and all the time you got on with your main job."

"No, that's total and utter—" Hanio tried to remonstrate.

"Don't try to deny it. You see, the ACS works closely with Country B. Ever since that code-breaking incident with the carrots, Country B has kept your name on their list as a Japanese police spy. You did some good work in that department, but that was your downfall. You ended up exposing yourself for what you really were. Everything was revealed. Everything. You stupid piece of shit!"

Smiling gently, the Asian pushed the sharpened tip of his pencil against Hanio's throat. "After that, we decided we wanted to investigate what your colleagues were up to. The best option would be to kidnap you immediately, extract your confession, and kill you. But by then we'd taken our eyes off the ball, and lost track of you. We were in big trouble. We couldn't leave things like that—we'd be compromised. At least, that's the way we saw it.

"Incidentally, that photo I took of you was invaluable. We made a huge number of duplicates from it. We had a good idea you'd start visiting your old haunts again in Shinjuku. So we got an LSD dealer, who works on the fringes of the organization, to distribute your picture and see if he came up with anything.

"He did the rounds asking all the bad girls to see if they knew the odd man in the photo who'd put a 'Life for Sale' ad in the newspaper. But he didn't find one who could tell him. You've slept with quite a few of the girls, but you're careful. Even those you have slept with had no idea of your present whereabouts. You'd moved out of your apartment.

"With a population of ten million, searching for a person in Tokyo is enough to make you throw your hands up in despair. There you were, someone who knew all about the ACS, hopping about like a flea somewhere in the city. And we had no idea how to catch you.

"But, my dear Hanio, it turns out that there are gods in the world. And the gods never abandon us. These gods love it when people create secret organizations. And in their infinite mercy they apply themselves in various ways on our behalf.

"The ACS has its roots in Hongbang, in China, and it was the local god of that district who helped us now. The name of this god is Great Ancestor Hongjun. Perhaps you've heard of him?

"During the Taiping Rebellion, a man called Lin was a commander in the army of General Zeng Guofan, which had gone to Yangzhou in order to quell the rebels. Lin was not very good in the ways of war: every time he led an army of thousands into battle, he lost. General Zeng was so enraged that Lin ended up being sentenced to death.

"Terrified for his life, Lin absconded with eighteen men under his command. They ran and ran. Eventually, they found an old mausoleum, where they settled down for the night. After a while they heard sounds outside: a large group of people seemed to be closing in. Thinking the end was near, they took up their weapons and stood at the ready, but then it turned out the crowd was not after their blood—they were just local villagers.

"These villagers told them: 'Just now, there was a big noise in the village. When we came out to look, a huge fire dragon was rolling about in the sky with its red flame lighting up the whole area as if it were daytime. Suddenly, it dived into the mausoleum. Convinced that some venerable personage must be staying here, we came to see.'

"Lin was relieved and asked the name of the village. He was astonished to hear it was a humble hamlet some fifteen or sixteen hundred miles away from the encampment that they had deserted earlier. In the space of a few hours, they had managed to escape this far.

"It was entirely thanks to divine assistance. In a framed picture hanging from the gate he saw the inscription 'Hongjun Mausoleum.' It would appear that their savior was Great Ancestor Hongjun. The following day they put together three gifts of fragrant candles, paper, and cloth respectively, along with water mixed with wine, and made an offering before the god. After that they all became virtuous bandits, robbing the rich and passing their wealth on to the poor. This is how it all started in Hongbang. I've digressed a bit, but I wanted to show how we came to worship that deity.

"And then the old guy happened to bump into you in a local park. Everything worked out fine in the end! We were able then to put a tracking device on you."

"It's exactly as he says." The old man nodded politely, looking as dapper as ever. Then he gave another glance toward Hanio with an apologetic expression.

"I can see how it makes total sense to you, but I'm telling you I have no connection with the police," Hanio remonstrated. "You have this paranoid superstition that everyone is a member of some organization. But all your talk about Hongbang is ridiculous: you really ought to get over it. In this world, people also exist who are unattached to any organization, who can live freely and die freely."

"Go ahead: say whatever you like while you can still talk," said the Asian. "And anyway, even Japanese police spies can say some sensible things. I'm fully aware they educate the police to quite an impressive level. But I haven't finished yet. After you removed the transceiver we shot into your thigh, you'd outwitted us again and we didn't know what to do. You're a real Houdini. You might have put your life up for sale, but you know, I've never seen a man who cares for his life as much as you do. At least until tonight.

"Can you guess how we knew you'd come to Hannō? We run travel companies that gather information on all traditional inns throughout Japan. We look after the guests at the inns, and in turn we gather information on them. My own travel company looks after its customers well, with a good reputation for excellent service, and the inns appreciate it a lot. The payback is that if some guest stays for a suspiciously long time, we get to know about it straightaway.

"We checked each inn in every region of Japan. We looked into the circumstances of every long-term guest roughly your age who was staying alone. Bit by bit we tightened the noose, until finally we worked out you must be the guy staying in the hotel by Hannō Station. And we were right. What a stroke of luck! Now, if we can catch a spy like you and bump you off after you've squealed, every other organization will be sure to reward us for it. No wonder everyone here today is so keen. All these foreigners are crazy about money.

"OK, I've got some questions. How many other police intelligence officers are investigating the ACS? Where do they operate? What are their activities? And how do they keep in contact with each other?"

Hanio suddenly remembered the black box in his pocket. He was pinning all his hopes on the apologetic expression in the old man's eyes.

54

"I understand. I understand." Hanio nodded. "So you're going to torture me to get information?"

"Exactly. And I'll also be getting some nice sketches at my leisure. I might put them together with the ones I made of you in action with Ruriko, and put on an informal private exhibition at some point. I think it would make an artistic, sensitive show. After all, it's only natural that people are born, love each other, and die."

"May I ask what you will do if I decide to kill myself before the torture begins?"

"Are you going to bite your tongue off?"

"No, I'll be taking the whole lot of you with me."

Hanio placed his hands, still bound with rope, on his jacket pocket, felt for the black box, and pressed the top of the stop-watch. A discernible tick-tock started up.

"You can hear that, can't you? The ticking sound . . ."

"What is it?"

Suddenly alert, the foreigners all rose from their chairs.

"Don't even think about pressing the trigger of that gun," warned Hanio. "The instant I see you move, I'll press this push-button switch, there'll be an explosion, and you, me, and everyone else'll be blown to smithereens."

"Don't you value your own life?"

"Say that again? I'm the man who put out a 'Life for Sale' ad. Don't for a moment put me in the same bag as all those other gutless spies. The bomb is now timed to go off in eight minutes. But if I press the button, it will detonate immediately. It'll blow this room apart, no problem."

Everyone tiptoed back, gingerly.

"Care for a look?" Hanio took out the sinister black box to show them.

This was the moment of truth. The box continued to tick away, sure and steady.

"Hey, wait! Don't you value your own life?" repeated the Asian.

"Fuck that! I'm going to be tortured and killed in any case. What's the difference?"

"No . . . Wait a moment. There is a way your life can be saved."

"What do you mean? Quickly then—spit it out. There are only seven minutes left."

"Become a member. We can discuss remuneration—we'll make it worth your while. So long as you don't disclose anything, you'll get social status, luxuries, women—everything you could need, Hanio, my boy."

"Don't 'Hanio, my boy' me. I don't want to join your stinking gang. As for myself, I lack any sense of morality, so I have no moral objections about what you do. It's all the same to me whether you kill people, or smuggle money or drugs or weapons. My only concern is to smash that misguided belief you seem to have that everyone you meet belongs to some organization. Plenty of people are not like that. Can't you see? And you've got to realize that there are also some who not only lack any affiliation, they also have absolutely no attachment to life. They may be few and far apart. But they certainly exist.

"I don't consider life valuable. My life is up for sale. I have no complaint about what happens to me. But I do take offense at being killed against my will, and that's why I'm quite prepared now to commit suicide. Even if that means taking the whole lot of you with me. Five minutes left."

"Wait. OK, how about us buying your life?"

"What if I tell you I'm not selling?" Hanio glanced briefly at the old man's face and raised the black box above his head.

As expected, the old man's response was immediate. He ran to the door and pushed it open.

"Come on, you lot. We should all make a run for it. We can leave him locked up alone in here. Let's just get out of here. If he wants to go and blow himself up, good luck to him. Come on. Let's scram."

"Four more minutes," said Hanio. He made himself comfortable in the chair and placed the black box on the nearby table, taking care to leave a hand resting on it. "If you go now, I won't detonate it immediately. I'll just wait for it to go off at the time set. That will leave me four minutes: some time to reflect on my life. You'd better run as far as you can—or you'll catch the blast. I wonder how far you can run in three or four minutes . . ."

Some hesitant slipping and sliding of feet on the floor was followed by a wholesale stampede through the door that the old man had left open.

Hanio watched them all go, then stood up quietly and shut the door. He walked to the other door, checked it was unlocked, opened it, and slipped out. Then, in an utter panic, he ran up the stairs as fast as his legs would carry him.

55

He was pretty sure no one would do anything flashy like take potshots at him from behind. He cut through the garden shrubs, got a foothold on the wall, and climbed straight over. Then he clambered down a bluff in a blind rush.

On the way down, he caught sight of lights flickering in the distance. He was surrounded by darkness, but a town lay just below. It seemed that the house was not exactly in an isolated mountain retreat.

He ran through the town, his body covered in bruises, shouting: "Help! Where's the police station?"

He ran, staggering, with both hands still bound. People he almost bumped into took fright and moved out of his way. They ignored him totally. Finally he heard someone shout in response: "There's a police station on the right, over there."

In the station, Hanio slumped to the floor, breathless, unable to speak. The middle-aged duty officer turned to look at him, bemused.

"Where have you come from?" the man asked calmly. "Oh, your hands are tied together. And you're injured."

"Where . . . where am I?"

"Ōme," the officer replied. He returned to his work.

"Water . . . Please give me water."

"You want water, do you? One moment."

The officer still continued leafing through his ledger. He finally laid down his old-fashioned fountain pen, put the cap on with care, and stood up. With one more glance at Hanio, he went to fetch some water. He showed no sign that he was about to untie him.

Hanio held up the cup of water, which brimmed with light, in both hands and then drained it dry. He never imagined anything in the world could taste so delicious.

The officer stole yet another look at Hanio's hands. He was probably apprehensive about what Hanio might try to do once he was freed. Hanio, with some reasoning power left, resisted the temptation to request that he be untied. There would be plenty of time later to complain about police negligence to a detective.

No sooner had this thought crossed Hanio's mind than the officer made a great fuss of untying his hands. Hanio realized his fears were groundless.

"What happened to you?" the officer asked, as if he were reproaching a son who had come home later than expected.

"I almost got killed."

The officer did not sound convinced. "What do you mean, you almost got killed?" Slowly, deliberately, he removed the cap from the fountain pen, took out a sheet of rough paper from the drawer, and began to write. He was dreadfully slow at writing.

Hanio was asked to provide a brief overview of what had happened, but he was dissatisfied to note that his words failed to elicit much of a response. He was, however, relieved when the officer finally picked up the telephone and reported the matter to the main station. Hanio seemed to have bumped his shins against something while he was clambering down the cliff: they were hurting a lot. Slipping his hand inside his trouser bottoms, he discovered that blood had already caked and turned sticky.

The response from the main station was taking its time. Meanwhile, the officer offered him tea and cigarettes, and was far more interested in discussing his own son than what had happened to Hanio.

"Our boy's at N— University. At least he hasn't joined some radical student union: that's a relief. But we do worry that he never studies at night, and all he ever seems to do is invite friends around to play mahjong. We're at our wits' end. His mother told him that, if he's going to be such a slacker, he may as well put on a helmet and swing a wooden bat around like one of those angry students on their demos. But then, what does he do but tell her that, since she's OK about it, he'll start demonstrating tomorrow. It's blackmail, plain and simple, and his mother doesn't know how to deal with him. Sons these days, they just rule the roost. But then again, I'm grateful that at least we've managed to get our kid into university. We've fulfilled our role as parents."

A few minutes later, Hanio saw the front lights of a bicycle approaching. A young policeman pushing the bike hailed them.

"This is the man." The officer introduced him with a few brief comments.

"OK, I'll take him from here," the policeman said bluntly.

The policeman walked his bicycle with Hanio, hardly acknowledging his presence. Hanio felt it necessary to keep an eye on his surroundings as they cut through the nighttime shopping district. The sound of music from some band blared out from a record shop. Hanio dragged his feet along as he walked, and fought against the occasional attack of dizziness.

When they reached the police station, a middle-aged

detective wearing a baggy suit came out and greeted him with unexpected warmth.

"Welcome to the station. OK, shall we take your written statement? This way, please."

He looked as if he had just finished dinner, as he repeatedly poked at his teeth with a toothpick. Hanio wondered if he should ask for a meal himself, but he was not at all hungry.

"Right then, in your own time. Let's begin with your name and address."

"I am of no fixed address."

"Oh."

The detective glanced at Hanio. He did not look pleased. His manner of speaking gradually changed.

"Now, both your hands were tied up, weren't they?"

"Yes."

"You do know it's possible to tie up your own hands, if you do it with your teeth."

"This isn't a joke. I almost got killed just now."

"That's terrible. Now, you say you came running down to the town, but where did you start running from?"

"From a residence on a bluff."

"If that's the area . . . It must be the bluff on the north side of town."

"I haven't any idea whether it's north or south."

"The chairman of K— Industries has a fancy home around there, and it's quite a smart residential street. You don't happen to know which house it was?"

"I didn't have time to read the nameplate."

"OK, forget that. Just give me the main details."

A long, tortuous conversation ensued. When Hanio started to race away with his story, the detective would raise his hand to motion him to speak more slowly.

"ACS? What's that?"

"The Asia Confidential Service."

"Asia Con-fi-den-tial Service. Is that a petroleum company, or something?"

"It's an organization that specializes in smuggling and murder."

"Got you." There were traces of a smile on the detective's lips. "What evidence do you have for saying that?"

"I witnessed it with my own eyes."

"You actually saw murder take place?"

"No, I'm not saying I saw it."

"How can you know if you didn't see it?"

"I'm sure you are familiar with the case of that woman, Ruriko Kishi. Her body was found floating in the Sumida River. We knew each other."

"Ruriko. Kishi. What character do you write Kishi with?"

"The same character that Prime Minister Kishi uses in his name."

"The Kishi from Prime Minister Kishi. Got it . . . She must have been a lovely woman. Was her corpse completely naked?"

"I believe it was."

"You're saying you didn't see that either?"

"I certainly saw her naked."

"In a nutshell, you had a physical relationship with her?"

"That's got nothing to do with it. She was killed by the ACS."

"Listen, young man." The detective suddenly put on an officious face and looked Hanio directly in the eye. "You keep mentioning the ACS, but do you have any proof that it actually exists? I won't waste my time taking down your statement. You come out with this name, ACS, that no one's ever heard of, claiming it exists. But my long years of experience tell me straight off that this is all a fabrication. The police force isn't here for you to come and tell crazy, made-up stories, you know. You've probably been reading too much weird detective fiction, but if you can't make your story stick, you'll end up getting charged with interference with a public official in the execution of their duties."

"You're being absurd. What would a policeman in the sticks like you know about it? Take me to the National Police Agency. I'll get a proper hearing from the people there."

"Oh, I'm so sorry that you've had to deal with a mere underling. But this underling's intuition works a hell of a sight better than that of his superiors, I can tell you. The sticks, what nonsense! You've got nerve, for a man of no fixed abode."

"So everyone without a fixed abode is suspect?"

"Yes, of course." Perhaps afraid that he might have gone too far, the detective softened his tone a little. "Respectable people all have homes. They devote themselves to providing for their wives and children. Surely I don't have to tell you that for someone your age to come here, single and homeless, makes you a dodgy member of society."

"Are you saying that every person must have an address, a home, a wife and kids, and a job?"

"It's not me that says it. It's society."

"So anyone slightly different is human trash?"

"You said it. It's not unusual for lonely men to suffer from delusions, and to come rushing into the police station to make false claims about being injured. If you think you're the only one, you're very much mistaken."

"Oh, really? In which case, you may as well treat me like a proper criminal. I've been involved in a very immoral business. I put my life up for sale."

"You did? Really? Boy, that must have been tough. But you're just the kind who would do that sort of thing. After all, it's not as if you did anything illegal. It's the one who buys another person's life and uses it for their own nefarious purposes who's the actual criminal. There's nothing criminal about putting your life up for sale. It's just that you just have to be human trash to do such a thing."

Hanio felt a distinctly cold sensation pierce his heart. He realized he would have to change tack and throw himself on the detective's mercy.

"I'm begging you. Please put me in a police cell, even if it's for a few days. Protect me! Someone really is out to get rid of me. I'll definitely get bumped off if some action is not taken. Please, I'm desperate."

"Don't be ridiculous. We're not a hotel, you know. From now on, just put aside your stupid ACS delusions."

The detective took a sip of his tea, by now quite cold, and turned aside in silence.

Hanio made one more tearful plea, but the policeman would have nothing of it. In the end, they threw him out through the front entrance of the station.

He was all alone. It was a glorious starry night. In a dark alley opposite the station he could see two or three red paper lanterns, probably signaling the local police watering hole. Night clung to Hanio's heart. It smothered his face, as if about to suffocate him.

Hanio could not manage even the few stone steps at the station entrance, so he sat himself down where he was. He took a bent cigarette from his trouser pocket and lit it. He was on the verge of tears, and a kind of twitching troubled the back of his throat. He looked up into the heavens. The stars blurred, and a myriad of lights blended into one.